Edited by Belinda Gallagher
Design by Oxprint Ltd

MY
AND L

ISBN 0 86112 639 4
© Brimax Books Ltd 1991. All rights reserved.
Published by Brimax Books Ltd, Newmarket, England 1991.
Printed in Hong Kong

# THS

# EGENDS

ILLUSTRATED BY

Roger Payne

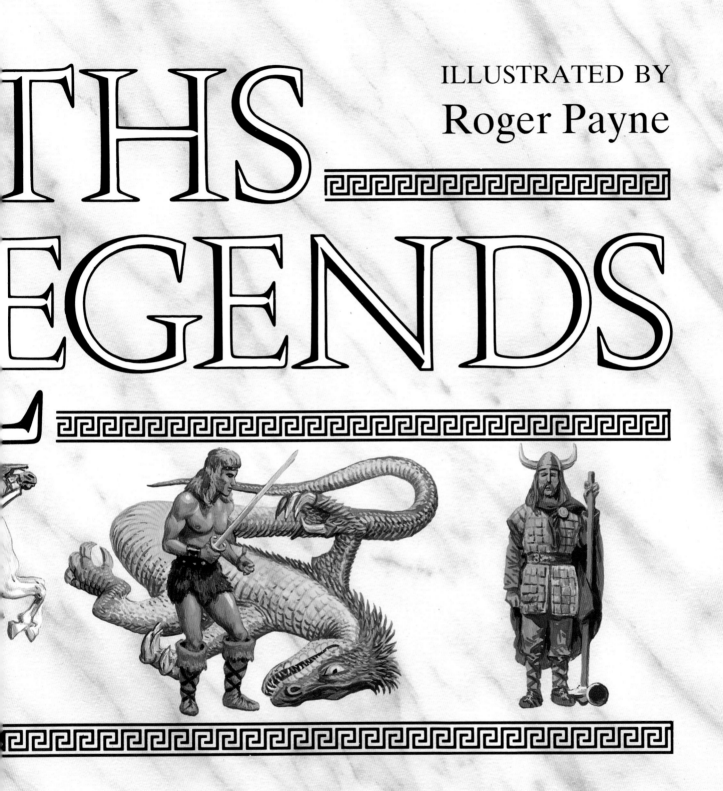

Brimax · Newmarket · England

Mythical monsters and legendary heroes have fascinated people for thousands of years. No one will ever know for sure if the terrible Minotaur ever existed or if the ancient Greeks really did destroy the city of Troy with a huge, wooden horse.

But behind all these fantastic stories there lies some truth. Perhaps the people within Myths and Legends really did exist, but over many, many years the stories surrounding them have become more and more outrageous until the true facts have all but disappeared. Whether true or untrue, Myths and Legends retells magical tales of fantastic feats and events that will captivate all who read them.

# CONTENTS

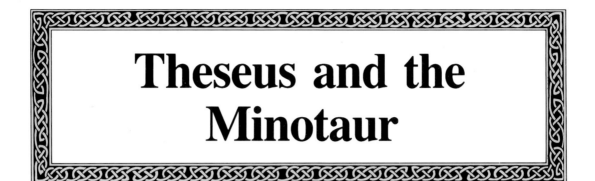

# Theseus and the Minotaur

It was very dark inside the tunnel. Only a little moonlight came in through the holes in the roof. It was cold, too. Theseus shivered.

Already, he could hear the monster, Minotaur, roaring and stamping inside the labyrinth. It sounded hungry and angry. But there were so many tunnels in the labyrinth that Theseus could not tell where the sound was coming from. He would have to go deeper into the labyrinth if he was going to find the monster and kill it.

Deeper into the labyrinth! What a frightening thought! No one who had entered the labyrinth had ever found the way out again. All had been killed and eaten by the Minotaur.

Theseus' fingers closed tightly over the ball of thread in his hand. His other hand gripped hard on the hilt of his sword. A sword, a ball of thread and, in the pocket of his tunic, a small golden phial. That was all he had to fight against the mighty Minotaur. The Minotaur was a bloodthirsty creature. It had the body of a man, but the head and the strength of a bull and fangs as sharp as a lion's.

No wonder Theseus' father, King Aegeus of Athens, had wept when he learned that his son was going to Crete to try to kill the Minotaur.

"I shall never see you again, Theseus," the King had said, tears streaming down his face. "Must you go? I am an old man. I need you here, to help me govern my kingdom."

Theseus was very sad to see his father so upset, but he could not do as he wanted.

"If I don't kill this monster," Theseus told Aegeus, "you will have to send more and more young Athenians to provide it with food every year. Just think how many have already died!"

King Aegeus sighed deeply. Theseus was right. The young people of Athens had paid a dreadful price. Years ago, King Minos' son had been killed in Athens. In revenge, Minos demanded that fourteen Athenians – seven young men and seven girls – should be sent to Crete. There they were fed to the terrible Minotaur. If this was not done, then Minos threatened

9

to attack and destroy Athens with his powerful army. However, if the young Athenians managed to kill the Minotaur, then Minos promised to stop demanding the yearly sacrifice.

'Oh, King Minos is cunning and cruel,' thought King Aegeus. 'He makes it impossible for anyone to kill the Minotaur by forbidding them to take weapons with them into the labyrinth.'

From the window of his palace, Aegeus could see the great ship with the black sail which made the sad journey to Crete every year. Aegeus saw fathers like himself weeping with terrible grief as they watched their sons and daughters climbing into the ship. Sadly Aegeus knew that Theseus must go with them.

"See how my people suffer!" sighed Aegeus. "If their children have to face the Minotaur, it is not right for their King to keep his own son safely at home."

Aegeus turned away from the window and said to Theseus, "We must say farewell, my son. I shall pray to all the gods on Olympus to protect you."

Aegeus picked up a small, golden phial that lay on the table nearby and gave it to Theseus. "This is from your stepmother, Medea. She says it will help you fight the Minotaur. As for me, I have one request to make of you."

"What is it, Father?" Theseus asked.

Aegeus gave him a large red square of material. "If you return safely from Crete, hoist this red sail from your ship when you come within sight of our shores."

Theseus smiled at his father, hoping to comfort him with cheerful words.

"My ship will have no black sail, Father," he told Aegeus. "This red sail will be flying from its mast when I return."

The voyage to Crete was a very sorrowful one. The fourteen Athenians could think only of the Minotaur and the terrible fate which awaited them. They wept and trembled. They grew more and more terrified as the ship approached its destination.

Theseus, however, was determined to show King Minos a brave face when he confronted him at his palace.

"What is the Prince of Athens doing here?" Minos demanded, recognising Theseus at once. "Surely King Aegeus has not sent his son to be sacrificed to the Minotaur?"

10

Theseus looked at Minos defiantly. "I have not come to be eaten by the monster," he answered. "I have come to kill it. Only then will my people be free from your terrible revenge."

At this, there was a great buzz of talk among the courtiers and nobles who surrounded Minos.

The King smiled a cruel smile. "Brave words, young Theseus," he said. "But the Minotaur is not so easy to kill when you have no weapons."

"I shall find a way to kill it," Theseus replied in a firm voice.

Princess Ariadne, King Minos' daughter, had been watching Theseus closely. Theseus was young, brave and strong, that was easy to see. Even so, he would need help if he were to succeed.

Ariadne made up her mind there and then that she would help Theseus in this difficult and dangerous task.

That night, Ariadne stayed awake for many hours until she was sure her father and his courtiers were asleep. Then she picked up a large vessel of wine and a ball of thread and crept from her room. Quickly and quietly, Ariadne passed along the corridors which led to the rooms where Theseus and his companions were staying. The sentries outside the doors were surprised to see Ariadne, but when she offered them some wine, they were pleased.

"The night is long and there are cold winds blowing here," Ariadne said, smiling graciously. "Some wine will warm you."

The sleeping drug which Ariadne had put in the wine took a little while to

work. A few minutes later, all the sentries were lying on the floor fast asleep.

Ariadne knocked quickly on the door of Theseus' room. He was surprised to see her and amazed when he heard what she had to say.

"I have come to help you, Theseus," Ariadne whispered. "Here, take this ball of thread, and a sword from one of the sentries."

"But why are you doing this?" Theseus asked in surprise. "Are you not afraid to anger your father?"

"My father is a cruel man," sighed Ariadne. "He feels no pity for those who die in the labyrinth! The only way to stop his cruelty is to kill the Minotaur . . . but we must not waste time! We must get to the labyrinth as quickly as possible."

Quietly, Theseus took a sword from one of the sleeping sentries and followed Ariadne out into the palace gardens and across the courtyard to the labyrinth. By the time they reached the entrance, Ariadne had told Theseus all he had to do.

A few minutes later, Theseus was inside the labyrinth. As he moved along the tunnel, Ariadne's ball of thread unrolled slowly on to the floor. The other end of the thread was tied to the inside of the door at the labyrinth entrance.

Theseus had not gone far before he heard the Minotaur roaring. He crept along a little further, letting the thread unravel in his hand. The next time he heard the roaring it was much nearer.

Theseus' heart thumped violently. 'Any moment now I shall see it!' he thought. Quickly, Theseus tucked the ball of thread behind a rock. Then he took the stopper out of the golden phial his stepmother had given him, and pressed himself back against the wall of the tunnel.

Suddenly the Minotaur was before him. It was roaring, stamping and shaking its great, thick fists at the roof of the labyrinth which imprisoned it.

"Ugh! It's horrible!" Theseus murmured in disgust. In the dim light, Theseus saw the Minotaur's wide shoulders, the sharp horns in its bull's head and its wild, glaring eyes.

The eyes were glaring straight at Theseus. With a tremendous howl, the Minotaur leapt at him. But before the monster could seize him, Theseus threw the powder from the phial directly into its face. The Minotaur bellowed as the powder filled its eyes and mouth. It staggered back, coughing. It pounded its eyes with its fists. For that moment, the Minotaur was helpless.

Theseus sprang forward. He swung his sword and slashed at the monster's legs. The Minotaur crashed to the floor, roaring in pain. It clutched wildly at the walls of the tunnel, trying to push itself on to its feet again. All the while, its jaws were snapping at the attacker it could not see.

Theseus stayed back and waited until the Minotaur had exhausted itself. At last, the monster lay gasping and panting on the floor. Its arms flopped motionless beside its hairy body.

12

Again Theseus leapt forward. He held his sword above his head. With all his strength he plunged the sword down and buried it in the Minotaur's heart. The Minotaur shrieked. Then the wild glare in its eyes faded. It was dead.

"The great gods be thanked!" cried Theseus, as he knelt beside the body of the monster. Suddenly Thesues felt pity for it. "It was not its fault it was born half-man, half-bull," he said. "Perhaps it is better for it to be dead than to live imprisoned in the labyrinth."

It was time to leave and join Ariadne, who was waiting outside. Theseus picked up the ball of thread from behind the rock where he had placed it. He walked back along the tunnel following the line of thread lying on the floor. Gradually, Theseus wound up the thread until at last he reached the entrance of the labyrinth.

When Theseus stepped out into the fresh, cool air of the night, Ariadne nearly cried with joy to see him.

"We must get away from Crete as fast as we can," Theseus told her. "You must come with us, Ariadne. If it became known how you helped us, you would be in great danger."

Ariadne nodded in agreement.

Swiftly, Theseus and Ariadne ran back into the palace, where the drugged sentries were sleeping. They roused the fourteen young Athenians and together they crept down to the harbour. When they ran on board the ship, the captain was amazed to see them.

"Get out to sea at once!" Theseus ordered. "Hurry! Hurry!"

It was still dark when the ship sailed out to sea and headed back to Athens but it was a joyful voyage, quite unlike the one that had brought the ship to Crete.

A few days later, Athens harbour came into sight. In the excitement of his victory over the Minotaur, Theseus forgot his promise to his father. When King Aegeus saw the ship flying the black sail, he thought Theseus was dead.

"I cannot bear to live any longer," he cried.

King Aegeus threw himself into the sea and was never seen again.

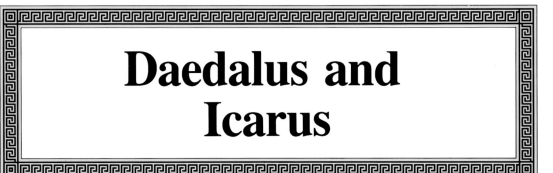

# Daedalus and Icarus

"Icarus! Wake up! Wake up!" Daedalus was sorry that he had to shake his son so roughly, but it was important that he woke up quickly. He and his father were in great danger. Any moment now, King Minos' guards would be outside the door. Daedalus shook his son again.

"Come on, Icarus!" he cried. "Wake up! By all the gods, why does the boy have to sleep so soundly?" Daedalus muttered. But then, everyone in the palace of Minos had been sound asleep the previous night when cunning Prince Theseus of Athens entered the labyrinth and killed the Minotaur imprisoned there. Everyone was fast asleep when Theseus sailed with the fourteen young Athenians who had come with him to the island of Crete. Moreover, Theseus had taken Princess Ariadne, King Minos' daughter, with him.

Next morning, when the King discovered what had happened, there was uproar throughout the entire palace. The first person the enraged King had called for was Daedalus, the craftsman who had made the labyrinth in which the Minotaur was kept.

"Where is that wretched Daedalus? Where is he?" King Minos raged. "I will tear him apart! I will burn him with hot coals! I will fling him off the cliff! The wretch, the liar! He told me that no one could get out of the labyrinth alive! Now the Minotaur is dead and Theseus has escaped with my hostages and my daughter!"

Daedalus heard the shouting and raving coming from the King's rooms and realised that the time had come to leave Crete – and to leave immediately! It was only a matter of time before Minos' soldiers came to arrest Daedalus – to drag him to the King.

Daedalus shook Icarus' shoulder again, more violently this time. Icarus opened his eyes and murmured sleepily, "What is it, Father? Why do I have to wake up now?"

"We have to escape, my son," Daedalus whispered urgently. "I will explain why later. But if we don't go now, it could mean death for both of us."

Icarus was wide awake now. His father was obviously worried, very worried indeed.

"You know you've always wanted to fly," Daedalus said. "Well, now's your chance."

Daedalus went over to a large box in the corner of the room. Somehow, Daedalus had always known that one day, he and Icarus might have to escape from Crete. So he had made wings from bird feathers, and set aside four balls of wax with which to stick them to their bodies.

Daedalus lifted the wings from the box and attached one pair on to Icarus' back. 'Poor Icarus,' Daedalus thought. 'He believes it's all a game.'

This was the second time he and his son had been forced to escape from danger together. The first time, Daedalus had to flee from his native city of Athens after he had thrown his nephew, Perdix, over a cliff in a fit of jealousy. Although Perdix was only a young boy, he was already a very clever inventor and craftsman. He was much cleverer, people said, than Daedalus himself. As Perdix tumbled over the cliff, the goddess Athene had saved him from death by turning him into a partridge.

Even so, Daedalus was afraid of what would happen when his crime was discovered, so he took Icarus and fled by night to the island of Crete. There, King Minos had given him shelter. Now Daedalus and Icarus had to run away again.

At last, Daedalus was satisfied with Icarus' wings. They were well fixed and should carry him safely across the sea. However, as Daedalus fixed his own larger wings on to his own back, he had a strong warning for Icarus.

"Remember your wings are stuck on with wax," Daedalus said. "Wax melts in heat, so take care not to fly too near the sun, or your wings will fall off! You understand, don't you, Icarus?"

"Oh yes, Father, of course I understand," Icarus replied, only half-listening.

Icarus was too excited at the thought of flying like a bird to think of anything else. The wings on his back were made of beautiful snow-white feathers, just like those of the birds he had often watched flying over the island. Already, Icarus felt very proud of them. With his great white wings, he would fly far better and further than his cousin Perdix, who had become a partridge. 'Partridges are only small, grey birds,' Icarus thought scornfully.

Daedalus looked at the eager, excited face of his son and prayed that no harm would befall him.

"Just follow me," he told Icarus. "Don't fly any higher than I do, and you will be all right!"

Just then, Daedalus heard a sound in the corridor outside. It was the tramp, tramp, tramp of soldiers' feet marching speedily towards his rooms.

"Quickly, Icarus!" Daedalus spoke urgently, as he led his son on to the balcony. "Jump up into the air when I tell you, and don't look down!" Daedalus gave Icarus a quick, anxious kiss, then said, "Now, Icarus! Jump!"

Icarus did as he was told and together with his father, he rose slowly into the air. The wings attached to his back moved up and down, and before long, Icarus and Daedalus were flying high above the grounds of the palace, over the golden sandy beaches along the shore and out to sea. The sun shone warm and bright around them, the sea below sparkled and the air felt fresh and clean on their faces as they flew along.

16

Every now and then, Daedalus looked round anxiously, to ensure Icarus was behind him. Every time, Icarus waved excitedly at his father. He was enjoying himself.

An hour or so passed. Below there was nothing to be seen but the sea and an occasional fishing boat. The island of Crete had long since disappeared below the horizon. By this time, Icarus was getting bored with just flying along behind his father. He wanted to do as the birds did – swoop downwards, turn and zoom upwards, perhaps move sideways in the wind currents that were blowing around him.

Icarus decided to try something. He glanced ahead to see that his father was not looking, then spread his wings out straight. He waggled them a little at the tips and found himself flying sideways.

"It works!" Icarus cried, in excitement.

Next, Icarus leaned downwards and swooped for a second or two, then zoomed upwards again so that he was once more flying behind Daedalus. Now Icarus could almost believe that he had never been anything but a flying creature.

Just then, a flock of birds came zooming up, right in front of Icarus. They were making for greater heights, before levelling out again. Icarus followed them. Up, up he went, hardly noticing that it was becoming hotter and hotter as he got higher and higher. The sun was shining more and more brightly, but Icarus did not stop.

"I can fly as high as the birds," he said. "I know I can."

Suddenly, far below, Daedalus turned round again. He found the sky behind him was empty. Greatly alarmed, Daedalus looked up and saw to his horror, that Icarus was nothing but a small dot high in the sky.

"Icarus! Icarus!" Daedalus cried out in great fear. "Icarus, come back!"

Icarus was far too high to hear him. Besides, he was feeling rather faint from the heat of the sun. He also grew more and more frightened as the wind currents took hold of him and shot him upwards at tremendous speed. Suddenly Icarus felt two burning patches on his back. The wax! It was melting! Suddenly, instead of flying, Icarus was falling. Below him as he fell, he saw his two wings being thrown about by the wind. They had come off.

Down, down Icarus plunged, faster and faster. Daedalus was turning this way and that, trying to see where his son was. Suddenly, the boy fell past him, arms flailing wildly, hands trying to clutch at the air. Daedalus turned cold with fear and grief. He was helpless. All he could do was to watch Icarus falling away from him, getting smaller and smaller until a splash of foam in the sea below marked the spot where he plunged into the water.

"Icarus, my son, my son!" Daedalus moaned. A dreadful ache entered his heart, for he realised Icarus could not have survived such a long fall into the sea.

Tears began to stream from Daedalus' eyes. He knew he had to find Icarus.

It was all too clear to Daedalus that Icarus was dead, as he flew down close to the level of the sea. He found Icarus' limp body floating on the surface. His face was terribly white and his eyes were closed. Floating nearby were the wings which had fallen from his back.

The weeping Daedalus gently lifted Icarus out of the water. There was a small, rocky island not far away. Daedalus flew to it and landed on a small patch of sand on the shore. For a few moments, Daedalus was unable to do anything but hold Icarus close to him and weep. At last, though, Daedalus realised that Icarus would have to be buried. With a grieving heart, he began to cover his son with rocks and stones from the sea shore.

There were many birds on the island and a small group of them perched on a rock nearby, as if they were watching Daedalus. One of them suddenly chirruped and, looking up, Daedalus saw it was a partridge.

'A partridge!' thought Daedalus. He looked more closely at the grey bird and remembered how his nephew Perdix had been changed into a partridge by Athene. Perhaps this partridge, looking at him now, was Perdix.

"If you are," Daedalus wept, "you will see how my crime against you has been avenged."

# Jason and the Golden Fleece

"So, Jason," said King Aeetes of Colchis. "You have come for the Golden Fleece!" Aeetes looked sternly at young Prince Jason of Iolcos, whose ship the 'Argo' had just sailed into the harbour at Colchis. "I must warn you that many have come before you, and all have failed. The dragon which guards the Fleece has killed every one of them!"

Aeetes hoped that Jason would be frightened by this warning. Some young warriors, who thought themselves very brave, had turned pale at the mention of the dragon. Others had found some excuse not to try to get the Fleece and very quickly left Colchis for home.

Jason was not like that. He had, in fact, solemnly sworn to fetch the Fleece and take it back with him to Iolcos. Only then would Jason's uncle, Pelias, keep his promise to give back the kingdom of Iolcos which he had stolen from Jason's father, King Aeson.

"I am not afraid, Your Majesty," Jason declared proudly. "I and my men, the Argonauts, have already braved many dangers to reach your land. We have faced huge giants, storms, winds and mighty waves at sea. The dragon which guards the Fleece cannot be more dangerous than these."

King Aeetes frowned. Jason was far too brave and confident for his liking. He was so brave and confident that he could well succeed where everyone else had failed.

The last thing Aeetes wanted was for Jason to take the Fleece. It was Aeetes' most precious possession. In any case, it belonged to Colchis and nowhere else. Many years ago, a prince called Phrixus had flown to Colchis on the back of a golden ram. After the ram died, Phrixus hung its fleece in the grove. He set a dragon to guard it, thinking the fearsome creature would keep the Golden Fleece safe from anyone who tried to take it.

Now Jason had arrived, it looked as if the Fleece was not so safe. Even so, King Aeetes was determined to keep it from him. So, he tried warning Jason again.

"The dragon never rests," he told the young Prince of Iolcos. "It watches the Fleece by day and by night."

"And I shall never rest," Jason answered, "until I get the Fleece from it."

Aeetes was furious at this reply, but he hid his feelings. Instead, he smiled and said, "If you are as brave in deed as you are in words, Jason, then the dragon will have much to fear. But come, let us talk no more of dragons and dangers. There will be plenty of time for that tomorrow. Now, you and your Argonauts must dine with me."

That night, King Aeetes was too worried to sleep. 'I must get rid of Jason,' he thought. 'I must think of a way to stop him taking the Fleece.'

All night, Aeetes walked back and forth, back and forth, in his bedchamber. All night, he plotted and schemed against Jason. Then at last, as dawn was breaking, Aeetes thought of a suitable plan.

"I'll give Jason three tasks," Aeetes decided. "Only after he has performed them all can he have the Golden Fleece!" Aeetes laughed out loud. "Jason will never perform the tasks," he chuckled with great glee. "They are all impossible! Each one is meant to kill him. He will be dead before he has finished the first – and the Fleece will be safe once again."

Unknown to King Aeetes, however, his daughter Medea knew of his wicked plans. Medea was a witch, with great powers. She was able to read her father's thoughts, even though her bedchamber in the palace was far away from his. What she learned greatly alarmed Medea.

She had fallen in love with Jason, even though she had never seen him before he arrived at the palace of Colchis the previous day.

"I must warn Jason," Medea decided. "With my magic, he can perform the tasks my father wants to set him. Without it, he will surely die!"

Medea hurried along the corridors of the palace to the room where Jason lay asleep. Without bothering to knock, Medea ran into the room and woke him up.

"Listen to me, Jason," she whispered urgently. "I have come to save your life!"

At that, Jason became very wide-awake.

"Who wishes to kill me?" he asked.

"My father, the King!" Medea replied, and briefly she told him of Aeetes' plans. The news made Jason very angry. He wanted to go and kill Aeetes there and then, before the treacherous King got the chance to kill him.

"No, no, Jason!" Medea told him. "I have a better way. Here – take this magic ointment. It will protect you while you perform the first task. For the second task, you will need this magic stone . . . "

"And for the third task?" Jason asked.

"Make sure your Argonaut, Orpheus is with you . . . and make sure he brings his lyre, the one that plays such beautiful music. Then the Golden Fleece will be yours," Medea said triumphantly.

Next morning, King Aeetes summoned Jason to his throne-room, and told him of the three tasks he had to perform.

"First," Aeetes instructed, "you must yoke two fire-breathing bulls to a plough and with them you must plough four acres of land. Next, you must sow the land with the teeth of dragons. A host of fierce armed men will at once grow from these teeth and you must kill them all!"

"I will do so!" Jason cried, pretending that he knew nothing of Aeetes' wickedness.

"Next," Aeetes went on, "you must kill the dragon in the magic grove. Only then can you take the Fleece home to Iolcos."

Shortly afterwards, a great crowd gathered in the fields outside the palace to watch Jason perform the first two tasks. King Aeetes was there and so was Medea. Apart from Medea, no one thought Jason had any hope of succeeding. Either the bulls would burn him up with their fiery breath or the host of armed men would kill him.

24

Jason came on to the field, clad in his finest armour. People in the crowd sighed and shook their heads, thinking what a pity it was that such a brave young warrior was soon going to die. What they did not know, of course, was that Jason had rubbed the magic ointment Medea had given him all over his body and his armour.

Suddenly, there was a great noise of hooves and the hiss of flames as two bulls came thundering into the field. Their eyes were fierce and with every breath, great blasts of fire leapt from their nostrils. Their hooves were made of white-hot metal and the ground steamed with heat as they trod on it.

'Soon, Jason will be burned to cinders!' thought King Aeetes gleefully as he watched Jason stride out towards the bulls. The next moment, though, Aeetes was glowering with anger as Jason marched into the flames quite unharmed. Because of Medea's ointment, he did not even feel the heat that surrounded him.

Jason grasped each of the bulls by one of its horns and with a quick movement, smashed their heads together. The animals fell to their knees dizzy and dazed. Quickly, Jason slipped a yoke over their heads, and waited for them to recover. When the bulls staggered to their feet, all their ferocity had gone and the fire in their nostrils and their hooves had cooled.

The bulls were now as meek as lambs, and they obediently pulled the plough across the four acres of land, with Jason directing from behind.

25

The crowd gasped in amazement at the sight. King Aeetes was furious. He wondered by what magic Jason had managed to perform this feat.

"Still, the next task will see the end of Jason," the King comforted himself.

Once again, though, Aeetes was disappointed and once again the watching crowd were amazed. Hundreds of armed men sprang from the dragons' teeth that Jason sowed. Jason hurled Medea's magic stone amongst them as she had told him. At once, the armed men turned on each other. They each accused the others of throwing the stone. They argued. They shouted. They began fighting among themselves. Soon, every one of them lay dead in the field from which they had grown only minutes before.

The crowd cheered and clapped and shouted with pleasure. They soon fell silent, however, when King Aeetes jumped to his feet and in a loud and angry voice called out, "Enough! Two such great tasks are enough for one morning! You must rest, Jason."

"But Your Majesty . . ." Jason protested.

Trembling with rage and frustration, King Aeetes interrupted him. "No! I have said it is enough! You can attempt the third task tomorrow."

'Tomorrow, my brave Jason, you and all your Argonauts will be dead!' Aeetes thought as he stalked angrily to his palace. As soon as he got there, Aeetes summoned the commander of his soldiers. He ordered him to kill Jason and his Argonauts as they slept in their rooms that night.

Medea, of course, was listening. At once she rushed to Jason and told him of this latest treachery planned by her father.

"You must get the Golden Fleece tonight!" she urged him. "Tomorrow will be too late!"

That night, Jason crept silently from his room, woke the Argonaut, Orpheus and with him crept out to the magic grove.

They saw the grove long before they entered it. The Fleece, which hung from a tree, shone so brightly that it filled the surrounding woods with brilliant golden light. It was so bright, that to Jason it looked like another sun shining inside the grove. Beneath it, his eyes watchful and unsleeping, sat the dragon.

"This must be the most fearsome dragon in the world!" Jason whispered to Orpheus, looking at the creature's thick, spiky tail and mouth full of sharp teeth. "But come, Orpheus. Sing."

Orpheus plucked the strings on his lyre and began to sing the most beautiful melody. When it heard it, the dragon pricked up its ears and stared in the direction of the sound. The music was so beautiful that the dragon's eyes lost some of their fierce expression. Then, as Jason watched and Orpheus continued to sing, the dragon opened its huge mouth and yawned. Its eyelids began to blink. It felt sleepy for the first time in its life. Then, its eyes closed and the dragon slumped down on the ground, fast asleep.

"Keep on singing, Orpheus," Jason whispered. Quickly he ran across the floor of the grove, sword in hand. Jason gave one great swipe with his sword and cut through the neck of the sleeping dragon. Then he scrambled up the boughs of the tree and unhooked the glittering Fleece.

Orpheus helped Jason stuff the Fleece into a sack. They did not want its golden light to give them away. Then they ran back through the woods and down along the narrow, tree-lined paths that led to the harbour of Colchis.

There, Medea and the rest of the Argonauts were already waiting in the 'Argo'. Jason and Orpheus jumped on board. The ropes that held the ship to the quayside were cut and the Argonauts rowed swiftly and silently out of the harbour. The wind filled the 'Argos' sails and by the time King Aeetes discovered what had happened, Jason, Medea and the Argonauts were far out to sea.

The triumphant Jason left one raging, furious King behind him in Colchis. Another King was just as furious when the 'Argo' brought Jason home to Iolcos.

Jason's uncle, King Pelias, had sent him to fetch the Golden Fleece believing the dragon who guarded it would kill him. Now that Jason had returned, Pelias was forced to keep his promise. He had to give back the Kingdom of Iolcos which he had stolen.

Once the wicked Pelias had gone, Jason brought back his father, King Aeson, from exile. It was a great day when Jason led his father to the throne in the palace of Iolcos, from which Pelias had driven him so many years before. That night there was a great feast to mark Jason's return and on the wall of the banqueting hall the Golden Fleece hung. It spread its brilliant light over a scene of great celebration.

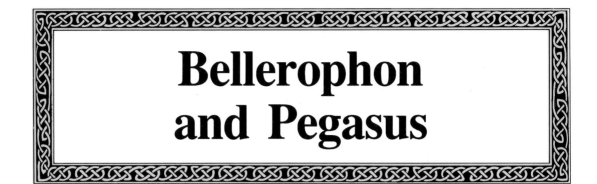

# Bellerophon and Pegasus

"It's Pegasus!" shouted Bellerophon.

At first, Bellerophon thought the reflection in the fountain was that of a huge white bird. When he looked up, he was thrilled to see it was a winged horse. It was the famous and beautiful Pegasus.

Bellerophon saw Pegasus glide down out of the sky on his silver wings. He landed on the bank near the fountain and began to drink. Bellerophon watched from his hiding place behind a nearby bush. In his hand, he held the magic golden bridle which the goddess Athene had given him.

"Pegasus is a wild horse," Athene explained. "No one has ever ridden on his back. But if you put this bridle on him, he will become tame."

Bellerophon had waited for Pegasus for many months. The winged horse did not come often to the fountain. Now Bellerophon could see the wait had been very worthwhile. With his powerful wings and strong back, Pegasus was a magnificent steed. He was the only horse strong and swift enough to carry Bellerophon in his great task of killing the monster, Chimaera.

Chimaera was a truly horrible creature. It had the head of a lion, the body of a goat and the tail of a serpent. It breathed fire and flames and for years it had been carrying off animals and small children. Chimaera's fiery breath burned down forests, fields of grain and whole villages and left them nothing but heaps of ashes.

Bellerophon had resolved to kill this dreadful monster, but he needed Pegasus to help him. First, though, he had to tame Pegasus. Bellerophon waited until the winged horse was chewing grass by the fountain. Then he ran swiftly towards him, took one great leap and landed on the horse's back. Pegasus was so alarmed that he launched himself into the sky at once. Up and up he went until he had taken Bellerophon above the clouds. Bellerophon clung on tightly all the way. Pegasus made tremendous efforts to dislodge him. He dived. He shot upwards again. He kicked his hind legs. He reared up. It was no use. Bellerophon remained firmly on his back.

31

Pegasus turned his head and tried to sink his teeth into Bellerophon's arm. That was when Bellerophon managed to slip the magic bridle over Pegasus' head and between his jaws. Just as Athene had said, Pegasus immediately became calm. He stopped throwing himself about the sky and now, when he looked at Bellerophon, all the wild fury had gone from his eyes. Instead, Pegasus gave his rider the look of an animal who knew and loved the man who was his master.

Bellerophon pressed his knees into Pegasus' sides. In response to this signal, the horse took him gliding down to the ground again. Bellerophon dismounted and went over to the spot where he had left the weapons with which he intended to kill Chimaera.

Then he climbed on to Pegasus' back once more and murmured, "Now, my splendid steed, let us seek Chimaera!"

It did not take long to find the monster. Bellerophon soon saw burnt and blackened fields below him.

'This is Chimaera's evil work,' he thought. 'The monster cannot be far away.'

Bellerophon saw it sitting on a mountain slope above the fields, grinning with satisfaction at the devastation it had caused.

"Chimaera has not seen us, Pegasus!" Bellerophon whispered. "We can surprise it. Now, my beauty, one of your swift, speedy dives – we must reach Chimaera quickly!"

Pegasus put his head down. As he swooped towards the Earth, Bellerophon held his bow firm and steady in one hand, and a bunch of arrows in the other.

"Slow down now, Pegasus," he whispered. Pegasus obeyed and slowed down until he was hovering just above Chimaera's head. Swiftly, Bellerophon fitted the first of his arrows on to his bowstring.

Just then, Chimaera looked up. A terrible hatred and fury glittered in its eyes and the lion's mouth opened to let forth a huge blast of flame and smoke. The flames shot up, almost enveloping Bellerophon and Pegasus in scorching heat. It was now or never.

Bellerophon released the first arrow, snatched up another, placed it in the bowstring and released the string a second time. Again and again, the bowstring twanged and a deadly shower of arrows began to pour down upon Chimaera. Soon, the monster was festooned with arrows and shrieking in pain. As it shrieked, flames blasted out of its lion's mouth. In vain, Chimaera threshed about, trying to shake off the arrows. Then it raised its head and shot huge tongues of flame at Bellerophon.

Bellerophon released the last of the arrows and told Pegasus, "A little higher, my beautiful steed. I must be out of reach of Chimaera's fire while I prepare for my final attack."

33

Obediently, Pegasus beat his wings faster and lifted Bellerophon up into the air, away from Chimaera's shooting flames. Bellerophon reached down to where a bag hung from his saddle and pulled out a huge lump of lead. He placed the lead on the end of his spear and made sure it was firmly fixed.

Bellerophon looked down to where Chimaera was hurling itself about in fearful pain. He was waiting for the moment when the monster looked up and tried to reach him again with its blazing breath. Bellerophon watched closely. Then came the moment he was waiting for. The lion's head started to move up.

"Take me down, Pegasus!" Bellerophon shouted.

Just as Pegasus reached the right spot above Chimaera, its head lifted up and its huge mouth opened. At once, Bellerophon plunged his spear deep into Chimaera's mouth. There was a ghastly sizzling and boiling sound from inside the monster's jaws. The monster gave a fearful, shrieking howl that pierced Bellerophon's ears.

"The lead's melting!" Bellerophon cried triumphantly.

He pulled the spear out and saw that the lump of lead had gone. The fire in Chimaera's mouth was so great that it had melted the metal. In dreadful agony, Chimaera rolled on to the ground and threw itself about as the lead flowed down its throat and burned its insides away. The monster's shrieks and howls got louder and louder, until at last, it gave one final shudder and lay still. Smoke began to rise from its dead body. Before long, fire broke through its hide and Chimaera was enveloped in a blanket of flame. The fire burned for a long time. Afterwards, all that was left was a pile of black, smoking ashes.

Bellerophon was thrilled at his tremendous triumph, but one thing spoiled his joy. Now Chimaera was dead, Bellerophon would have to set Pegasus free. They had faced great danger together and Bellerophon had come to love the beautiful winged horse.

Bellerophon felt so sad when he removed the magic bridle and told Pegasus, "Now you can roam the skies as freely as you did before."

Pegasus did not move.

"You are free," Bellerophon repeated. But instead of flying away into the sky, as Bellerophon expected, Pegasus came to him and brushed his mane against his shoulder. Bellerophon was delighted. He knew what the winged horse was trying to say.

Pegasus did not want his freedom. He wanted to stay with his master – and of his own free will.

# Perseus and the Gorgon

King Polydectes of Seriphos was feeling very pleased with himself. At last, he had managed to get rid of Perseus. The boy was a nuisance. Ever since he and his mother Danae had been shipwrecked on Seriphos, Perseus had protected her against the King. Polydectes, who hated both of them, wanted Danae as his slave. Determined to have his way, the King had tried for years to find some means of sending Perseus to certain death. Now he had succeeded.

"Perseus is a fool!" Polydectes laughed with wicked satisfaction. "He fell straight into my trap."

Polydectes' trap was simple. He invited Perseus to a banquet. The guests were supposed to bring some rich gift with them, but Perseus was so poor that he had nothing to give.

"You must wipe out this insult, Perseus!" Polydectes demanded, pretending to be very angry. "You must bring me the head of the Gorgon, Medusa! Swear you will do so!"

Perseus had to do as the King demanded. However, the task he swore to perform was not only difficult – it was impossible!

"Perseus cannot kill Medusa without looking directly at her," Polydectes chortled gleefully. "The moment he does so, he will be turned to stone!"

While King Polydectes was congratulating himself on his cleverness, Perseus was feeling desperate.

'What am I to do?' he thought. 'I don't want to be turned to stone but I can't kill Medusa with my eyes shut!' Perseus knew now that the King wanted him dead, but he could not go back on his word. That would be a dreadful disgrace.

"I am doomed," Perseus decided gloomily. "There is no escape!"

Happily, Perseus was wrong. The Greek gods Athene and Hermes had seen and heard all that had happened. They were watching from the Palace of Olympus where the gods lived high up in the clouds.

"Perseus is in terrible trouble," sighed Athene, the goddess of wisdom. "We must help him."

"Of course we must," replied Hermes, the messenger of the gods.

Hermes thought for several moments. Then at last he cried, "I've got it! Come, Athene, bring your shield which shines like a mirror. I'll bring my curved sword and a pair of my winged sandals."

"Where are we going?" asked Athene.

"To see Perseus," Hermes told her. "On the way we will call on Hades in the Underworld, and borrow his helmet of invisibility. Then we will go to the Nymphs and borrow their magic wallet. Come, Athene, we must hurry. There is no time to lose."

Suddenly, or so it seemed to Perseus, a bright, golden light started shining in front of him. Perseus was dazzled by it. Gradually, he was able to make out the shapes of the tall, beautiful Athene and the small, slim Hermes.

"Who are you?" Perseus asked, mystified by these creatures who shone with golden light.

"We are beings with great powers," said Athene. "We can do things humans find impossible."

"Like killing Medusa," Hermes added, with a smile. "Or at least telling you how it can be done!"

Perseus frowned. "You are making fun of me," he said suspiciously. "No one can kill Medusa without being turned to stone first!"

"You are wrong, Perseus! You can do it," replied Hermes cheerfully. "Here are the things you will need."

Perseus stared in amazement as Athene and Hermes laid before him Athene's shield, the helmet of invisibility, the magic wallet and Hermes' curved sword and winged sandals. "What use are all these things?" Perseus asked.

37

"Listen!" replied Hermes. The wings on his sandals flapped as he flew up to whisper in Perseus'ear. As Perseus listened to Hermes, he stopped frowning with worry. By the time Hermes had finished, Perseus was very cheerful and excited.

"Marvellous! Wonderful!" he cried, as Hermes fluttered back to the ground. "Now I can kill Medusa and get her head!"

"All you need to know now is the way to the Land of the Dead where Medusa and her two sisters live," said Athene.

"Don't you know it?" Perseus asked in surprise.

"Only the Old Grey Women have that knowledge," Hermes told him. "They are strange creatures with only one eye between them, but it is so powerful that it can see to the end of the world."

"What are we waiting for?" Perseus cried impatiently. "Let's go and ask them!"

Hermes put his hands under Perseus' elbow. Slowly, Perseus felt himself rise into the air. The wings on his own sandals were beating up and down like the wings of a bird. Perseus had never flown before and at first he wobbled a bit. Soon though, he was flying as swiftly and as surely as Hermes.

A few moments later, they were flying over a seashore and Hermes was pointing to a large cave close by the beach.

"There they are!" Hermes cried.

Perseus looked down and saw the three Old Grey Women coming out of the cave. Together with Hermes, he swooped downwards to land on the shore. At once, Hermes darted behind a nearby bush and signalled Perseus to do the same.

As the Old Grey Women approached, they were arguing fiercely.

"You've had the eye long enough now, Sister," croaked one Old Woman. "Let me have it. I want to take a look at the world."

"No, it's my turn," protested the Woman behind her.

The two blind Women were groping about, but the one with the eye avoided them. "You will both have to wait," she said. "I haven't finished with the eye yet."

"They always quarrel like this," Hermes whispered. "Wait until the Old Woman with the eye gives it to one of the others. Then all three are blind. Here's what you must do . . . "

Perseus waited until the Woman with the eye took it from the hole in the centre of her head and began passing it to one of her sisters.

"Now! Quick!" cried Hermes.

Perseus leapt up, rushed over to the Women and snatched up the eye. The Women shrieked with alarm.

"Who's there?" they cried. "Someone's stolen our eye!"

"Your eye is quite safe," said Perseus. "I have it here!"

"Give it back! Give it back this instant!"

"Not until you have told me how to reach the place where the Gorgons live!" Perseus said firmly.

The Old Grey Women whined and complained, but they knew that without their eye, they were all helpless. At last, they gave in. One of the Old Women angrily told Perseus all he wanted to know.

"Now," snarled the Old Woman when she had finished. "Give us back our eye!"

39

Perseus placed the eye in the forehead of the Old Woman who had spoken to him. As soon as she could see again, she tried to scratch him with her long, black fingernails. Perseus escaped by rising swiftly into the air on his winged sandals. Hermes went with him.

"We must part here," Hermes said. "Farewell, Perseus. Remember all you must do when you reach the land of the Gorgons."

Hermes soared into the clouds and out of sight. Perseus turned westwards, as the Old Women had said and flew past all the coasts and oceans which they told him led to his destination.

Beneath him as he flew, the Earth looked like a carpet of many colours. There was the dark green of the forests and grasslands. There was the gold of the sand on the seashore, and the blue of the lakes, rivers and oceans.

After a while, though, Perseus could see only black rocks and grey barren mountains. Perseus knew he was nearing his destination. At last, he saw a large, black island below. Three shapes lay on the rocks by the shore. They looked like giant, winged dragons.

"The Gorgons!" Perseus cried, feeling frightened and excited at the same time.

All three looked as if they were asleep. When he looked at them, Perseus shivered with horror.

The Gorgons were the most horrible creatures he had ever seen. From their cheeks grew two white tusks. Their hands had long claws made of brass. Two Gorgons were covered in dragon scales from head to toe. The head of the third Gorgon, instead of hair, was a mass of writhing snakes.

"That must be Medusa," breathed Perseus.

He had to hurry. The Gorgons might wake at any moment. Perseus hovered in the air, while he placed the helmet of invisibility on his head. He opened the magic wallet that hung from his belt and gripped Hermes' curved sword in his right hand. Then, with his left hand, Perseus carefully moved Athene's mirror-like shield until he could see Medusa's reflection in it.

40

Slowly, Perseus flew down towards the rock where Medusa lay, keeping her reflection in the shield all the time. He was nearly there – lower, then a little lower. Perseus was above Medusa's head.

'Now!' he thought, and with one swift stroke, he brought the curved sword down. Its tip clanged on the rock as it sliced through Medusa's neck. Perseus darted downwards, using the shield like a mirror to show him what to do. Quickly, Perseus grasped Medusa's head and pulled it off the sand where it had fallen. He pushed it into the wallet and fastened it tightly.

Just then, the other two Gorgons woke up. When they saw Medusa's headless body lying on the rock, they let out dreadful screams and howls. But they could not see who had killed her. The helmet of invisibility Perseus was wearing made sure of that.

It was time to escape. The wings on Perseus' sandals beat rapidly and he soared up into the air, leaving the two Gorgons screaming and clutching vainly at the air.

Perseus began his long journey back to the island of Seriphos. At last he flew down to land on the beach near Polydectes' palace.

A few minutes later, Perseus marched into the palace. Before anyone could stop him, he threw back the doors of the banquet hall, where Polydectes was feasting his nobles. Everyone jumped in surprise.

When Polydectes saw that Perseus had returned, he went pale with fear.

"I have the Gorgon's head, Polydectes," Perseus said in a confident voice. "I have done as I promised."

Despite his fear, Polydectes laughed. "Come, now, Perseus!" he said. "How could you have killed Medusa and returned alive?"

By now the nobles of Seriphos had also recovered from their surprise.

"You lie, Perseus!"

"You're talking nonsense!"

"It is impossible!" These cries rang out from all round the hall.

Then Polydectes signalled to one of his servants. "Go, fetch the mother of this foolish boy!" the King instructed. "Bring Danae and let her see her son is a liar!"

When Danae entered the hall, Perseus found it hard to recognise her. Polydectes had forced her to do all the dirty jobs in the palace kitchens. She looked old and worn.

When she saw Perseus, Danae's eyes shone with tears of joy. But Perseus was horrified to see how the King had ill-treated her.

"Keep your eyes on the floor, Mother," Perseus whispered to Danae. "Don't look at what I am going to do!"

Danae did as Perseus told her. Then Perseus turned again to King Polydectes. "You want proof that I have killed Medusa?" he demanded.

"You haven't got any proof!" cried Polydectes.

"Very well, look at this!" Perseus replied and pulled Medusa's head out of the magic wallet.

Immediately, King Polydectes and his nobles turned into stone. Some had their mouths open in amazement. Others were holding up their hands to shield themselves from Medusa's terrible eyes. It was no use. They all became solid grey stone in an instant.

Perseus plunged Medusa's head back into the wallet and closed it. He put his arms round Danae and embraced her. She was gasping with amazement at the hall full of statues.

"We are free from the wicked King," Perseus told her. "He will never trouble anyone ever again!"

# Achilles and Hector

"Achilles! Achilles! Come quickly!" Patroclus was shouting loudly as he ran through the Greek camp. He had dreadful news. The Trojans were attacking the Greek ships and throwing burning torches on to the decks. Dozens of Greeks had already been killed.

If Achilles had been there to fight them, the Trojans would not have dared to be this bold. However, Achilles was not there. After his quarrel with Agamemnon, the Greek leader, he had refused to fight and retired to his tent.

Achilles looked up, startled, when Patroclus burst into his tent. "Our ships and our men are in terrible danger," panted Patroclus. "You must save them, Achilles."

Briefly, Patroclus told Achilles what had happened. Then he added: "We have not fought Troy for nine years to lose the war now! Only you can save us."

"No," growled Achilles. "I will not come!"

"But Achilles . . ." Patroclus protested.

"Agememnon insulted me," Achilles said gruffly. "I will not help him now!"

Patroclus fell to his knees in despair. "Then all is lost," he moaned.

Since Achilles had retired to his tent to sulk about Agamemnon, many Greeks had come to him begging him to return to the fight. Achilles had refused them all. He found it hard, though, to turn Patroclus away as roughly as he turned away the others. For Patroclus was his dearest friend. They were like brothers. So, when Achilles saw Patroclus weep in despair, he gave in just a little.

"I will not fight, Patroclus," Achilles repeated. "But I will help."

"How?" cried Patroclus, suddenly hopeful again.

"I will lend you my armour," Achilles told him. "When the Trojans see it, they will think I have rejoined our men."

This was marvellous news. The Trojans feared Achilles more than any other warrior on Earth.

Quickly, Achilles helped Patroclus buckle on his shining armour. Patroclus felt proud to be wearing it.

Achilles, however, had two warnings for him. "If you succeed in driving the Trojans away from our ships, do not pursue them back to Troy. And keep away from Hector!" Achilles added sternly. "He is the greatest of the Trojan warriors. Only I can match him in battle."

"I will remember," Patroclus promised.

"Make haste, then, and may the gods protect you, dearest friend," Achilles said.

Riding in Achilles' chariot, Patroclus sped back to the battlefield. He arrived to find the fighting was more savage than ever. The sky overhead was black with smoke from the burning Greek ships. The shore was littered with the bodies of dead Greeks and their upturned chariots. The air was filled with the ringing sounds of swords clashing with spears, and the shouts and cries of men locked in fierce contest.

However, when the Trojans saw Patroclus disguised in Achilles' armour, they became terrified. They broke off the fight and began speeding their chariots towards their city of Troy and safety.

"After them! After them!" cried Patroclus. He was so excited, he forgot Achilles' warning.

Patroclus and the Greeks set off at tremendous speed. Their chariots threw up clouds of dust as they chased the fleeing Trojans. They drove so fast that when they came within sight of Troy, the Trojans were still some distance from the city.

"We're catching up!" Patroclus cried in triumph.

Just then, a Trojan turned his chariot round and began driving back towards Patroclus. Patroclus recognised him at once.

"It's Hector!" he gasped. It was too late, Patroclus remembered Achilles' second warning. Frightened, Patroclus flung his spear at Hector's chariot. It missed.

When the rest of the Greeks saw Hector's chariot thundering towards them, they loosed a shower of arrows. They failed to stop him. Hector drove straight at Patroclus and with one blow struck him on the side of the neck with his sword. Achilles' armour stopped the blow from killing Patroclus, but his helmet and neckplate were knocked to the ground.

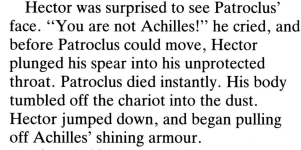

Hector was surprised to see Patroclus' face. "You are not Achilles!" he cried, and before Patroclus could move, Hector plunged his spear into his unprotected throat. Patroclus died instantly. His body tumbled off the chariot into the dust. Hector jumped down, and began pulling off Achilles' shining armour.

When Achilles learned that Patroclus was dead, he gave a terrible howl of grief. He was so overcome with sorrow that he fell to the floor of his tent. He pounded the earth with his fists. He sobbed. He cried out his friend's name. He wept again and vowed to get his revenge.

"Hector!" Achilles suddenly shouted in a thunderous voice, as if to make the Trojan warrior hear him. "You shall die! And after death, you shall be punished."

That night, Achilles did not sleep. He could think of only one thing: he must kill Hector and avenge his lifelong friend Patroclus. Hector also remained awake. He knew that when he met Achilles it would be in the most savage battle he had ever fought.

That night Hephaestus, the god of fire and industry, was busy making Achilles a fresh suit of armour to wear in his battle with Hector.

Next morning, Achilles found the armour in his tent. He put it on and came out, fully armed and armoured for battle. The Greeks were very pleased to see that Achilles had at last returned to fight by their side.

When the fighting started that day, Achilles fought like a madman.

After a few hours, the Greeks could no longer count the number of Trojans Achilles had killed.

All the time, Achilles was looking for Hector. It was late in the afternoon before he saw him. By that time, the Greeks had fought their way up to the walls of Troy. The Trojan warriors were rushing back into the city and guards stood ready to close the gates as soon as they were all inside.

Hector, however, refused to come in. He stood outside the gates, waiting for Achilles. His father, King Priam, came on to the battlements and begged Hector to seek safety within the walls of Troy. Hector's mother, Hecuba, and his wife Andromache, also came and pleaded with Hector. Hector would not listen.

Then Hector saw a great flash of brilliant light not far away. The last rays of the afternoon sun had struck Achilles' brilliant armour. Nearer and nearer it came, until Achilles could be seen thundering towards Hector in his chariot at tremendous speed. There was a terrible look of hatred on Achilles' face as he saw Hector.

Achilles' chariot swept towards the waiting Hector, and as it came close, Hector threw his spear. Achilles saw it coming, and raised his shield. The spear hit it, bounced off and clattered to the ground. At once, Hector drew his sword and came rushing towards Achilles. Achilles jumped from his chariot and sprang towards him, with his spear outstretched.

"Die as Patroclus died, vile Trojan!" Achilles snarled. His spearhead went through Hector's neck. With a dreadful choking sound, Hector fell to the ground, dead.

There was a cry of horror from the battlements above as Priam, Hecuba and Andromache saw Hector fall. But their horror and grief grew even greater when they saw what happened next.

Achilles took his dagger and cut through Hector's feet from the heels to the ankles. He pushed a rope through the holes and fastened the end of it to his chariot. Then Achilles leapt into his chariot, whipped the horses into a a gallop and began dragging Hector across the ground. Faster and faster the chariot went with Hector's body trailing behind it. Soon the body was torn, battered and black with dust.

Each day for many days after that, Achilles returned to the walls of Troy with Hector's dead body trailing behind his chariot. Day after day, King Priam wept bitterly at the dreadful spectacle.

At last, Priam could bear the sight no longer.

'I must forget I am a King, and humble myself before Achilles,' he thought.

The grief-stricken Priam left Troy and went to the Greek camp, taking with him many magnificent gifts. The gifts would be Hector's ransom, or so Priam hoped. When he entered Achilles' tent, Priam threw himself before the great Greek warrior.

"Have pity on me!" Priam wept. "Have pity, great Achilles! Give me back my dead son."

For a while Achilles said nothing. He seemed stern and unyielding. Priam pleaded with him again. He even kissed Achilles' hands, which is what servants did to show obedience to their masters.

At this, Achilles looked down at Priam's lined, old face and his sorrowful eyes, which were swollen and red with weeping. Suddenly, Achilles remembered his own father, Peleus.

'If Hector had killed me,' Achilles thought, 'my father would have wept for me in the same way.'

The remembrance of his own father made Achilles take pity on Priam at last.

"Do not kneel to me, old man!" he said. "Do not weep! The body of your son shall be washed and clothed, and you shall return with it to Troy."

Achilles kept his word. Priam received the body of Hector and took it home to be properly buried.

As he watched Priam leave, Achilles knew that the gods on Olympus would punish him for the dishonourable deed he had committed. He knew, too, what the punishment would be.

'I shall be killed here, at Troy,' Achilles thought. 'I shall never return home to my father, and he will not be able to bury my body, as Priam will bury Hector's.'

Not long afterwards, all this came true. Achilles was killed by Paris, Hector's younger brother, and his father never saw him again.

# The Wooden Horse of Troy

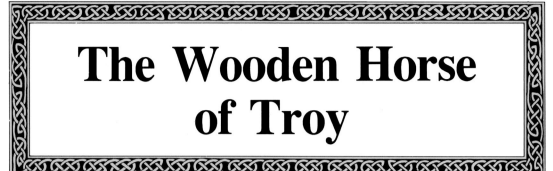

The Greeks had gone. After ten long years of war and seige, it seemed that they had given up and left Troy in peace. The Trojans could hardly believe their eyes when they saw the Greek ships sailing away. It was amazing.

Just as amazing was the strange wooden horse they had left behind, standing just outside the city walls. Was it a gift or was it a trick?

King Priam of Troy certainly suspected that the wooden horse was some kind of trick.

"The Greeks are the most cunning people on Earth," Priam warned the Trojans. "We must be very careful!"

Priam knew that some Trojans thought the horse was a sign of luck and victory. They wanted to drag it inside the walls of Troy. Priam forbade them to do so until scouts had gone out to make sure the Greeks really had gone home.

The scouts armed themselves with swords and spears, in case they ran into a Greek ambush. Then they slipped out of the city to investigate the place where the Greeks had made their camp. There was no ambush. What was more, there was no camp. When the Trojans reached it, they found the Greeks had burned their huts and tents. All that remained were a few heaps of blackened wreckage.

While the scouts were picking their way through the ruined camp, they discovered one solitary Greek man trying to hide behind some bushes. They dragged him out, kicking and shouting, and threw him on the ground.

"I beg you, do not kill me!" he shrieked. Then he started moaning. "Oh, what misfortune has overtaken me! How unlucky I am!" As he wailed and lamented, the Greek man wept so much that the Trojans began to feel sorry for him.

"Who are you?" they wanted to know. "Why have the Greeks gone and left you behind?"

"My name is Sinon, and the Greeks hate me!" the man sobbed. "When they realised they could never capture Troy, they decided to go home. They feared the gods would think them cowardly, so they sought the advice of the oracle . . ."

"What did the oracle say?" asked the Trojans curiously.

"The oracle said that the gods would not think the Greeks were cowards if they left behind one man as a sacrifice," Sinon continued. "I am that sacrifice. Agamemnon, our leader, never liked me and as for Odysseus – the cunning, cruel man – he often said he wanted me killed! Now they have got their way."

Sinon had stopped weeping now, and his tears had been replaced by fury and resentment. "They have betrayed me!" he cried. "Well, I will betray them!"

Sinon got to his feet and gripped one of the Trojans by the arm to make him pay close attention. "I will tell your King everything," Sinon promised. "I know the secret of the wooden horse. I will reveal that secret, but only to King Priam."

When Sinon mentioned the wooden horse, the Trojans pricked up their ears.

"Let's take this wretched Greek to Priam," the Trojans' leader decided.

"No, there's something odd going on," protested one of the scouts. "I don't trust this fellow – let's kill him now!" He looked Sinon up and down with fierce, suspicious eyes. Sinon trembled and cringed before his gaze.

"Look at him!" the Trojan leader replied. "A man as terrified as this can be no danger to us. Besides, he has been betrayed and wants revenge. Such a man will always tell the truth."

Sinon buried his face in his hands and started to make loud weeping noises once again. Unseen by the Trojans, Sinon was smiling behind his hands. 'The plot is working,' he thought. 'Everything is going exactly as Odysseus planned.'

If the Trojans had any suspicions left about the departure of the Greeks, those suspicions soon vanished after Sinon told his story to Priam.

"The Greeks built the wooden horse as a gift for the goddess Athene," Sinon explained. "See the smiled carved upon its face. The Greeks put it there to turn away Athene's anger. They were afraid she would send storms to wreck their ships as they sailed home . . . but here is the really cunning part of their scheme . . . "

"What? What?" asked Priam, longing to know. Everyone in Priam's court strained their ears to hear what Sinon had to say.

"The Greeks were certain that you would burn the horse when you found it, thinking it was some trick on their part," Sinon went on. "If that happened, then the fury of Athene would fall on Troy and she would send a great thunderbolt and a cloud of fire to burn down this beautiful city."

"So the wooden horse was a trick after all," said King Priam. "We shall show the Greeks we are not fools here in Troy. We shall treat this horse with respect and honour. Bring it inside the city. We will hold great celebrations round it." Priam clapped Sinon on the back in a friendly fashion. "We have much to thank you for, Sinon. You shall join us as an honoured guest."

Sinon chuckled secretly to himself. Of course, everything he had told King Priam had been a lie – except that the Greeks had indeed despaired of winning the war. That at least was true.

"If we cannot defeat the Trojans by force of arms," Odysseus told the other Greeks, "we must defeat them by cunning. Listen – I have a plan."

When Agamemnon, the Greek leader, heard Odysseus' plan, he ordered his army to take their axes and chop down trees in the forest on nearby Mount Ida. Then Epeius, the Greeks' most skillful carpenter, got to work with his men. He cut the trees into thousands of planks and set about constructing the wooden horse. It took Epeius three days to complete it.

As soon as the horse was ready, Agamemnon gave orders for the Greek camp to be burned. While the ships in the nearby harbour were made ready for the sea, Odysseus, Epeius and a number of Greek warriors put on their armour. They wrapped their swords and spears in their cloaks.

When it grew dark, they climbed up a long ladder and entered the hollow belly of the horse, through a trap-door in one side. When everyone was inside, Epeius pulled up the trap door and bolted it. There they sat, in the darkness, holding their weapons tightly so that they did not rattle while the horse was hauled to a spot outside the walls of Troy.

Then Agamemnon and the rest of the Greeks, all except Sinon, embarked into their ships and sailed away. Sinon was left behind in the camp, waiting for the Trojans to come and find him.

The Trojans were so completely convinced by Sinon's story that they flung open the city gates and hauled the wooden horse inside. A crowd followed behind singing, dancing and cheering.

'They think they have won the war,' Sinon thought. 'They will soon discover they have lost it!'

51

At length, the Trojans grew tired and started to go home. Sinon stayed behind. When the last Trojan had disappeared, he ran swiftly to where the wooden horse stood and gave three raps on one of its legs.

"At last!" murmured Odysseus in the darkness of the horse's belly. "The time has come for action!"

Odysseus and his companions unwrapped their swords and spears. Epeius crawled to the trap-door, unbolted it and let it down. He drew out the ladder and carefully lowered it to the ground. Within a few minutes, all the Greeks had climbed down and two of them sped swiftly to where Trojan sentries stood guard in front of the main city gates. The sentries were dozing. They had had too much wine to drink during the celebrations. Suddenly, the Greeks were upon them. Two swift thrusts with their daggers, and the sentries were dead.

52

This was the moment for Sinon to climb the staircase to the ramparts. He carried a torch in his hand. Sinon waved it back and forth over his head. Far away, across the water, he saw an answering signal: a torch, like his own, moving from side to side. It was a look-out on the Greek ships. The ships had not sailed out to sea, as the Trojans thought. They had simply sailed out of sight round a nearby headland.

The rowers pulled hard on their oars and the Greek ships began to move back towards Troy. Inside the city, the Greeks were pulling the gates open.

Agamemnon and his soldiers were soon pouring into the city, and before long Troy was filled with shouts and screams and the crackle of burning buildings. The Greeks burst into the King's palace and killed Priam and his family. Others ran through the streets, swords in their hands, slaying every Trojan they could find. Others threw flaming torches into the houses and horrible screams were heard from within as the people inside burned to death.

Soon the streets of Troy were strewn with the bodies of the dead and the whole city was covered in thick, black smoke. Men, women and children were running about shrieking in terror. There was no escape. They were killed or bound in chains and dragged to the ships.

By the time dawn came, the once splendid city of Troy was nothing but a smoking, silent ruin. No one was left alive.

When the Greeks finally left, carrying off their prisoners and all the gold and treasure they had looted, the only structure left was the wooden horse. Untouched by the flames, it stood in the square, smiling a triumphant smile.

# Odysseus and the Cyclops

"What's that?" said Odysseus, waking up in alarm. He was sure he had heard some creature bellowing and thumping about close by. The cave where he and his twelve companions – all Greeks – were resting was echoing from the noise. Odysseus listened. There it was again – a dreadful sound that seemed to make the whole cave shake.

Lying beside Odysseus, snoring contentedly, was his companion Eurylochus. Odysseus shook him until he opened his eyes.

"What's the matter?" Eurylochus muttered sleepily.

"I thought you said this cave was empty – that no one lived here!" Odysseus hissed fiercely.

"It looked as if no one did," Eurylochus replied, surprised to see Odysseus so furious. "We were so tired after our voyage here, to the island of Sicily. I chose the first cave we found to shelter for the night."

"You may soon be sorry you were not more careful," Odysseus told him. "There is some horrible creature nearby. Listen!"

Eurylochus strained his ears and listened hard. He heard nothing. All was quiet. Obviously Odysseus had made a mistake. Eurylochus opened his mouth to say so. In the next moment, it stayed open – but in horror and amazement.

For a deep, rumbling roar reached Eurylochus' ears from outside the entrance to the cave. It was so loud that it woke up the eleven other Greeks who were with Odysseus. They all sat up, shaking with fright.

"What is it? What is it?" they cried.

"It sounds like some horrible giant!" said one of the Greeks, his voice trembling.

It WAS a giant. As Odysseus and his men stared fearfully at the cave entrance, two enormous feet thumped down just outside. They made a noise like thunder. Each foot was bigger than all the thirteen men put together.

Horrified, they all looked upwards – past the giant's colossal knees and legs as thick as tree trunks, past the giant's enormous torso, until they were looking at the ugliest, most ferocious face they had ever seen.

"That mouth – look at it! It's as big as the gates of Troy!" one of the Greeks gasped.

The enormous cheeks were as big as the walls of Troy, and the giant's hair hung down on either side of them like two long, thick curtains.

Then Odysseus and his men saw the eye. Just one eye. It was set in the middle of the giant's forehead. The eye was looking straight at the thirteen terrified men.

"By all the gods on Olympus!" Odysseus cried. "It's the Cyclops! It's Polyphemus!"

Polyphemus was famous for one thing: he liked the taste of human flesh. Odysseus' men knew this. They scrambled to their feet and rushed towards the back of the cave, hoping to find somewhere to hide. There was nowhere.

Polyphemus was inside the cave now. He towered high above the Greeks, with his head almost touching the roof.

"I have been out hunting for my food," Polyphemus bellowed with great satisfaction. "But I come home to find it waiting for me, instead!"

Before they could jump out of the way, Polyphemus reached out with his enormous hand and snatched up six of the Greeks. As they struggled and screamed, Polyphemus opened his huge mouth. Odysseus watched, horrified, as the six Greeks disappeared into the giant's mouth. One crunch, and they were gone. Polyphemus licked his lips with satisfaction.

Odysseus wept with grief and rage. The six men who had just died so horribly had lived through so many dangers. Together with Odysseus and the others, they had survived the ten long years of the war the Greeks had waged against Troy. After the Greeks destroyed Troy, they set off on the long, hazardous sea journey home. On the way, they survived many storms. One storm had brought their ship here, to Sicily. Now, in the cave where Odysseus had thought to find rest and warmth, the six men had made a meal for the dreadful Cyclops.

"Why do you weep?" A big, booming voice sounded in Odysseus' ears. He looked up to see Polyphemus glaring at him. "Is it because I have eaten your friends?" Polyphemus asked. "Do not weep! You shall soon be with them!"

With that, Polyphemus snatched up Odysseus and the remaining Greeks, three in one hand and four in the other. Polyphemus' eye looked from one handful of men to the other. The Cyclops seemed to be making some decision.

Then, to their great relief, the Cyclops said, "I have changed my mind. I have had enough food for now. I shall keep you until later. In the meantime, make me a fire to warm myself. A big one!"

Odysseus and the six Greeks found themselves down on the ground again. There was a heap of firewood on one side of the cave. The Greeks hurried over to it and began piling it up to make a fire.

"We must find a way to get out of here," Odysseus whispered to his companions. "Let me think. Fire! Even Polyphemus can be hurt by fire."

Meanwhile, Polyphemus went outside the cave. He returned carrying the long pole he used as a walking stick and a huge jar full of wine. A flock of sheep followed the Cyclops into the cave. Odysseus saw a big pile of sheep's skins lying in one corner.

"I know what will happen to these sheep!" he sighed.

Then an idea entered his mind. He knew how the sheep could help them all escape!

The fire was burning warmly now. Polyphemus lay down beside it and held up his huge hands to warm them.

"This is well done," he said. "You humans may be tiny, puny creatures, but you have made a good fire."

Odysseus pretended to be grateful. "We only seek to serve you, Polyphemus," he told the Cyclops. "Let us bring you some wine."

57

Polyphemus smiled. "A fine idea," he boomed. "Since you are so small you can bring me the wine in those buckets over there . . ." The Cyclops pointed towards the other side of the cave.

Odysseus and his companions began filling the buckets from the huge jar of wine.

"There is enough wine to fill a lake here!" Odysseus whispered. "We must see that Polyphemus drinks it all."

It took a very long time to make Polyphemus drunk, which is what Odysseus wanted. The Greeks tramped back and forth carrying bucket after bucket of wine. Polyphemus drank them all. When all the wine was gone, Polyphemus became very sleepy. At last, his one eye closed and he lay snoring on the floor.

"Quickly!" Odysseus whispered to the others. "Let's get the Cyclops' walking stick."

Between them they heaved the stick off the floor, using all their strength. They dragged it towards the fire and held its pointed end in the flames until it grew hot.

"Good!" said Odysseus. "Now let's lift it up . . . Come on. Higher! Higher!"

Then, when they were holding the stick high enough, Odysseus told them, "Plunge it in his eye. Ready? Now!"

They ran forward together and thrust the heated end of the stick into Polyphemus' closed eye. There was a frightful smell of burning and scorching. Polyphemus let out a ghastly yell of pain. He clapped his hands to his eye, shouting and bellowing. The Greeks were almost deafened by the noise.

"Why is it so dark?" roared Polyphemus. "I can see nothing!"

Polyphemus started to feel the walls and the floor of the cave. He was looking for Odysseus and his companions. His huge fingers kept thumping down close to them. They were big enough to crush them.

Odysseus ran over to the pile of sheep's skins. Swiftly he threw one to each of his companions. "Cover yourselves with these, and get down on your hands and knees!" he cried. "Then start crawling towards the door of the cave."

Quickly the Greeks did as Odysseus told them. Suddenly, Odysseus felt the Cyclops' fingers feeling along the sheep's skin that covered his back. The fingers felt like a colossal weight. Polyphemus felt another sheep's skin, then another and another. Each one covered one of the Greeks.

"They have escaped!" Polyphemus bellowed. "Those cunning humans! They have blinded me and escaped. Only the sheep remain here in the cave."

As swiftly as they could, Odysseus and his companions crawled out of the cave. Once outside they threw off the sheep's skins which had saved their lives and ran towards the shore.

"The ship is too badly damaged to sail," Odysseus said quickly. "But the small boats are all right. Quick! Launch them and let us get away from this island."

The Greeks quickly pushed the boats out from the shore. Once they were afloat, they started to row them out to sea as fast as they could move the oars.

Many more adventures awaited Odysseus and his companions before they reached Greece and home. However, they always remembered the night they escaped from the Cyclops as the most dangerous and fearful of them all.

# Horatius at the Bridge

"They're coming! They're coming!" The sentry's cry of warning echoed down from the watchtower high above the city of Rome. The sentry hurried down the staircase to report to the commander of the Roman army, Lucius Junius Brutus.

"A thousand, perhaps fifteen hundred men . . . " the sentry told Lucius breathlessly. "Spearmen, swordsmen and horsemen. A league away, I should say – perhaps three thousand paces."

Lucius turned to face the rows of soldiers who stood before him, armed, armoured and ready to fight.

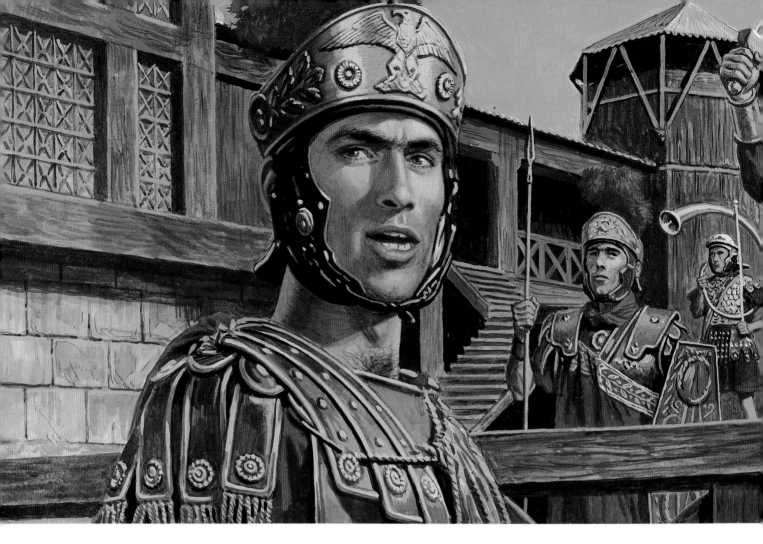

"You have heard the news," Lucius told them. "King Tarquinius and his ally, King Porsenna of Clusium, are coming with a great army. Tarquinius wants his throne back – he wants to become King of Rome again and rule us as harshly as he did before! Will we allow him to succeed?"

"No! No!" The soldiers' reply came in a great roaring shout. "We have had enough of kings! We threw Tarquinius out of Rome – he can stay out!"

Lucius smiled. He felt proud to be the leader of an army with such courage and spirit. Lucius knew that his commanders – young men like Horatius and Gaius Mucius – were fine leaders, and the troops they were to lead were great fighters. What more could any leader of an army ask?

'Still,' thought Lucius, 'it will not be easy to defeat Tarquinius and Porsenna.'

One thing was certain. The enemy must not get across the Sublican Bridge over the River Tiber. If that happened, Rome could be in great danger and its earth ramparts might not be enough to stop Tarquinius from entering the city.

That was why Lucius had ordered Horatius and his men to stand guard on the Sublican. If anyone could keep that bridge safe and secure, it was Horatius.

Suddenly, a dreadful howling sound reached Lucius' ears. A moment later, a huge boulder came thudding down to earth, and landed about twenty paces outside the ramparts. The attack had begun and the enemy was using stone-throwing and other siege machines.

"To your posts!" Lucius yelled to his army. He drew his short sword from its scabbard and raised it above his head. "Fight to the death for Rome!" he cried.

As the soldiers ran to station themselves along the ramparts, Lucius nodded to Horatius and Gaius Mucius. It was the signal the two young Roman commanders had been waiting for. Horatius clasped Gaius by the hand.

"Death to Tarquinius!" Horatius said firmly. "The gods preserve you, Gaius, my friend!"

"The gods preserve you, Horatius," Gaius replied. "You greatly need their protection."

Gaius was right, Horatius thought, as he led his fifty men out of the city, and down the Palatine Hill towards the Tiber and the Sublican Bridge. The gods of Rome would have to fight very hard on his side, for defending the bridge was a truly perilous task. It had no proper defences. All Horatius and his men could do was to stand and fight with the River Tiber and the bridge behind them.

The bridge was made of thick, strong wooden planks. Many times since it was first built by Ancius, fourth King of Rome, the bridge had been swept away by floods. This was not one of those times, however. The Sublican stood strong and firm as Horatius marched across, and the river flowed quietly beneath it.

"Spearmen, over there – swordsmen on this side!" Horatius quickly ordered his men to their positions. He concentrated half his force at the end of the bridge, and stationed the rest along the banks of the river on either side.

The army of Tarquinius and Porsenna was very close now, so close that Horatius could see the designs emblazoned on their shields. Horatius tried to count the number of enemy soldiers, but there were too many of them.

Suddenly, Horatius heard the whistling sound of a spear slicing through the air towards him. He jumped aside to avoid it and the spearhead struck the bridge and stuck there. A swordsman was making straight for him, yelling fearful war cries and brandishing his sword in the air. Horatius leapt forward, thrusting his own sword up and the two swords met with a loud metallic clang. There came a scraping sound as the swordsman whipped his sword away. He wielded it again to strike another blow at Horatius, but before he could do so Horatius lunged forward and plunged his sword into the man's chest. The man gave a horrible gurgling cry and crumpled to the ground.

Quickly, Horatius looked round. Along the bank of the river, fierce struggles were going on, with two enemy soldiers or more lunging at each Roman with swords and spears.

The air was filled with the sounds and the screams of battle, the clash of sword on sword, the whistle of javelins flying through the air and, from some distance in front of Horatius, the heavy clank and thud of the enemy's siege machines. Several times, Horatius saw huge boulders and stones flying through the air above his head. The boulders fell into the river behind him, but Horatius realised what the enemy was trying to do.

'They're trying to kill us all quickly – one of those boulders could crush five men,' Horatius thought anxiously.

For the moment, the aim of the men working the siege machines was not accurate. All their missiles fell into the Tiber or on to the opposite bank of the river.

If they shortened their range a bit or pulled their siege machines back a little . . .

Then it happened. A great boulder came whistling over and hit its target – half a dozen of Horatius's spearmen who were holding a group of enemy soldiers at bay with their javelins. There was a dreadful crash and terrible screams as the spearmen were crushed down onto the ground by the enormous weight.

Suddenly, Horatius smelled burning. He looked quickly along the river bank. Several Romans, their clothing ablaze, were leaping into the water in an attempt to put out the flames. It was obvious what had happened. The siege machines were now being used to fling burning torches.

Then Horatius saw something even more horrifying. Not one of his fifty men was left standing. Their bodies were strewn on the ground or floating in the river or sprawled out on the banks sloping down to the water.

Horatius was alone – the only man left out of his entire force!

"Very well, then!" Horatius cried. "If that's how the gods have decreed, I'll defend the bridge alone!"

Horatius snatched up a javelin lying nearby, and leapt a few paces back along the bridge. There he stood, sword in one hand, javelin in the other, with his shield looped firmly round one arm. Horatius snarled at the crowd of enemy soldiers in front of him. "But that one man is a Roman! You shall not cross this bridge, I swear it!"

The enemy soldiers were so startled that for a moment they did not move. Then one of them began to laugh.

"He's mad!" he yelled. "Imagine one man against all of us!"

Other soldiers took up the cry and started to yell insults at Horatius. "You're a lunatic!" they shouted. "You'd best jump in the river and cool your crazy head!"

Horatius stood his ground, his eyes dark with fury and determination. "You shall not cross!" he growled. He lunged at one enemy soldier who was just about to jump on to the bridge in front of him. The enemy retreated hastily, back to the safety of the crowd at the end of the bridge.

Horatius realised that the soldiers were afraid of him. They thought he was out of his mind, and feared to fight against a madman. It could not go on for much longer though. Someone would throw a spear or a sword, and that would be the end.

Fortunately, Gaius Mucius had seen what was happening from the ramparts above. He ordered his men to open the gates so that they could go to Horatius' aid.

"Fetch some axes!" Gaius ordered. "There's only one way to save Horatius – and Rome. We've got to chop that bridge down."

Horatius' position was getting very dangerous now. As Gaius and his men rushed out of the gates and started running down towards the bridge, one of the enemy soldiers lunged at Horatius with his sword. Horatius managed to twist the sword out of the man's hand and throw him back. Gaius knew it would take only seconds for Horatius to be overwhelmed, if the enemy came at him in force.

Reaching the bridge, Gaius started to hack away at the planks that held it to the river bank. Four or five others were doing the same. Gradually, the planks were cracking and splitting apart. Horatius felt the bridge vibrate and as the first four planks were chopped through, the whole bridge began to sway. The enemy soldiers saw what was happening and drew back from their end of the bridge, fearful of being thrown into the water when it collapsed.

Gaius and his men kept chopping away at the planks, turning the blades of the axes to split the wood, until only one plank was left. By now, the bridge

was swaying alarmingly. Gaius gave a terrific swipe with his axe and as
the blade chopped through the last plank, the bridge suddenly tipped sideways.
With a great creaking, groaning and splintering it toppled down towards
the river. Horatius was flung off. He plunged into the water and disappeared,
weighed down by his heavy armour. For one dreadful moment, Gaius thought
Horatius had drowned. Then suddenly, there he was, up on the surface again
and swimming strongly towards the river bank. Gaius rushed forward and
grabbing Horatius' hand, hauled him out of the water.

"There," Horatius told Gaius, pointing to the confused horde of enemy
soldiers who were staring at the wrecked bridge. "I told them they wouldn't get
across."

All along the ramparts, the Romans were cheering and shouting out
Horatius' name. When he came back into the city, Lucius Junius Brutus was
there to congratulate him for his magnificent deed. Lucius placed a laurel
wreath on Horatius' head and told him, "This is the mark of a hero of Rome.
You will be among Rome's greatest heroes, Horatius. Tarquinius will never
come back now that he has Romans like you to contend with."

Lucius was right. After seeing what had happened at the Sublican Bridge,
King Porsenna, Tarquinius' ally, became afraid to fight against the Romans.
Porsenna went home to Clusium, leaving Tarquinius with no soldiers to fight
for him.

Tarquinius had lost his throne for ever, and never again were the Romans
ruled by Kings.

# Androclus and the Lion

**A**ndroclus shivered as another icy drop of water dripped on to his face. He looked up at the cave roof above his head. Another drop plopped down on to the rocky shelf beside him.

Androclus drew his cloak round his shoulders and wrapped his arms round himself trying to keep warm.

It was no use trying to sleep in this cave, he thought miserably. At least the soldiers who were out hunting for him would not find him in here, and maybe the lions would not find him either. Well, Androclus hoped so. The last thing he wanted was for a ferocious lion to come into the cave. The animal would probably be hungry, and then . . . Androclus did not want to think about what would happen.

'At least I'm free now,' Androclus thought, trying to cheer himself up.

One thing he knew for certain – his cruel master, Publius Sirius, would not be able to give him a beating today and then send him off, sore and aching, to do a day's hard labour in his vineyards. Androclus had hated his master ever since the day Publius had bought him in the slave market in Rome.

Four years passed before Androclus managed to escape from Publius's farm. Now, hiding inside the cave, Androclus thought over the plans he had made to get away from Italy. He would stay in the cave until it grew dark. The soldiers Publius had sent to catch him would not be looking for him at night. Then Androclus planned to leave the cave and make his way to the coast. There, he hoped to find a boat and sail back to his home in Greece.

Androclus looked at the shafts of light that were coming into the cave. The sun seemed to be low in the sky now. It might be dark soon.

"I must have a look," Androclus murmured. He peered out of the cave entrance. "Good," he said seeing the deep blue of the sky. "An hour or so, and the sun will set."

Suddenly, as he was turning to go back into the cave, Androclus saw the lion. His skin prickled with fright. He gave a start as a low, growling roar came from the lion's throat. It stood only a few metres away from him. It was a powerful creature, with a flowing mane and a great swishing tail. There was something strange, though. Surely the lion would have noticed Androclus by now?

However, it seemed to be more concerned with its front paw, which it was holding off the ground and licking from time to time. Every now and then, the lion gave a sort of whining howl, as if it was in pain.

When Androclus looked at the paw, he saw why. It was very swollen and rather black in colour. Quite obviously, it hurt a great deal. Androclus felt great pity for the wounded creature. He wanted to help, but it was a great risk.

Androclus was very soft-hearted. He loved animals and could not bear to see even a fierce lion suffering. His mind was made up quickly. Moving carefully, Androclus approached the lion. The lion was sitting down now, whining and licking its paw. As it heard Androclus creep closer, it looked up. Androclus saw that instead of the wild, ferocious glare lions usually had, this one was looking at him pleadingly, as if it wanted help.

Very slowly, Androclus stretched out his hand and stroked the lion's mane. To his relief, the lion let him do it.

"That's a bad paw you've got there, poor old fellow," Androclus murmured. "Let's have a look at it – all right, I won't hurt you!"

The lion gave a howl as Androclus touched its paw. For one terrible moment, Androclus thought it was going to attack him. But it looked sadly at Androclus and the howl became a whine. Androclus carefully lifted the lion's front leg and lookcd closcly at the injured paw.

There was a large, sharp spike embedded in one of the pads. It looked like a large thorn, or a piece of metal.

"That's got to come out," said Androclus. It was best to do it quickly. Androclus grabbed the spike and pulled hard. As he did so, the lion gave a deafening roar.

Androclus went back into the cave to fetch some water from one of the many puddles that lay on the floor inside. Androclus tore his cloak into two long strips, soaked them in the ice-cold water and went outside again.

For the next few minutes Androclus bathed his swollen paw and wrapped it up in the long, wet-strips of cloth. All the time, the lion watched him. Now and then it let out a sound rather like a purr. After a while, the swelling in the paw seemed to go down a bit and it did not look quite so black as before. Androclus felt thankful, too, to see that there was less pain in the lion's eyes.

Finally, he made a pad out of one of the wet strips of cloth, placed it over the wound and then wrapped the paw in another strip.

"That will protect it until it heals," he told the lion. 'In a strange way,' Androclus thought, 'the lion seems to understand.'

The lion was obviously feeling a lot better. It got up on three legs and began to hobble around. It hobbled forward a few steps and before long, the lion was moving along the rocky path, away from where Androclus stood watching it. Then the lion began to move more quickly until it disappeared over a small hillock.

What Androclus did not know as he watched the lion was that three soldiers were watching *him*. They had spotted Androclus outside the cave and crept up unseen while he was tending the lion. Now the soldiers were hiding behind rocks further up the hill, waiting until the lion disappeared from sight.

"All right," one of the soldiers muttered to the others when the lion had gone. "Let's grab him!"

Androclus heard the soldiers as they scrambled from behind the rock, but by the time he started to run away, it was too late. One of the soldiers grabbed Androclus round the waist and threw him on to the rocky ground. The other two held him down, while the soldier tied his wrists together with rope.

Androclus felt like weeping. It was so unjust that his act of kindness towards the lion should end like this.

One of the soldiers gave Androclus a rough push.

"Your master, Publius Sirius, wants to see you," he told Androclus. "He's got a very special punishment for runaway slaves!"

"What is it? What's going to happen to me?" Androclus gasped, knowing how cruel Publius Sirius was.

The soldiers laughed. "You'll see!" they sneered. "And when you do, you'll be sorry you ever thought of running away."

71

Three weeks later, Androclus sat on the floor of a large underground cellar with his hands chained to a ring that was sunk into the stone wall. Nearby sat another man, chained in the same way, and next to him, another. From above their heads, they could all hear the crowd chattering and laughing in their seats around the amphitheatre. From the excitement in their voices it was clear that the crowd expected good, blood thirsty sport. After all, it wasn't every day that runaway slaves and ferocious lions were put into the arena together. Emperor Tiberius himself was coming to watch.

This was certainly a special punishment, just as Publius Sirius had planned. 'This time,' Androculus thought grimly, 'there is no hope of escape.'

There was a sudden burst of cheering from above, in the amphitheatre.

"The Emperor's arrived," the man next to Androclus whispered. "It won't be long now!"

A few moments later, the bolts on the cellar door were drawn back and the door creaked open. A troop of soldiers marched in and started unchaining Androclus and the other slaves. They were pushed into the centre of the cellar and a large grille at the end was pulled up. Beyond it lay the sand-covered arena, the eagerly awaiting crowd of spectators – and the lions. Androclus felt a sharp push in his back and he stumbled forward. With the other slaves, he emerged into the brilliant sunshine that filled the arena. As the crowd spotted them, they let out a great yell of excitement.

72

There was a scraping sound from across the arena and a grille at the opposite end moved up. At once, ten or twelve lions came bounding out and started racing across the sand to where the slaves stood, petrified with fear.

The first lion to reach them leapt upwards and Androculus got a quick glimpse of the underneath of its belly as it landed on a slave and knocked him to the ground. Androclus and the rest of the slaves started to run. They ran out into the centre or round the sides of the arena.

The crowd shouted and clapped as they watched. They laughed at those slaves who tried to climb the walls in an attempt to escape, only to have lions leap up at them and pull them back.

Suddenly, Androclus saw a lion leap towards him. He tried to get out of the way, but the great animal was upon him before he could do so. Androclus felt the hot pain as the lion's claws tore into his arm. Any moment now, and Androclus would feel the lion's sharp, curved fangs sinking into his flesh . . .

73

But nothing like that occurred. Instead, to Androclus' amazement, the lion started licking the scratches on his arm. The crowd saw what was happening, and their shouts of excitement turned to shouts of astonishment.

When the lion had finished licking Androclus' arm, it lay down next to him and put its paw across his chest, as if to protect him.

Even the Emperor Tiberius was on his feet, mouth wide open with amazement. Nothing like this had ever been seen in the amphitheatre before. Androclus put his hands up and turned the lion's face towards him.

"I know you," Androclus said. "And you haven't forgotten me."

The lion purred as Androclus lifted its paw and looked at it. There, sure enough, was a small, round hole in one of the pads. This was the lion Androclus had tended at the cave. Now it was showing how grateful it was. Not only had the lion not killed Androclus, but it was growling fiercely at the other lions.

The whole amphitheatre was in an uproar now. The Emperor ordered the animal keepers to drive the other lions back into their cellar. The slaves who were unharmed stood and wept with relief at their unexpected escape from death.

Androclus got to his feet, and dusted the sand off his tunic. The lion sat meekly beside him, looking up at him with adoring eyes. Everyone in the crowd was clapping. Even the Emperor joined in, and a tremendous cheering broke out as Androclus walked round the ring with the lion following him like a faithful dog.

Emperor Tiberius was so amused that he gave Androclus his freedom.

"A man who can tame the wildest of beasts cannot be a slave," the Emperor told the delighted Androclus.

Androclus was even more delighted when the Emperor let him keep the lion as his own. Afterwards, the two of them became well known in Rome. Wherever Androclus went, the lion went too. No one was afraid to meet them in the street, even when Androclus did not put the lion on a lead. After all, wasn't it the tamest lion ever seen in Rome?

# Rungnir and Thor

There was great shouting and fury in the Palace of Jotenheim where the great Norse Giants lived.

"You are a fool, Rungnir!" some of the Giants were shouting. "You have agreed to fight the great god Thor! You are mad, quite mad!"

"Thor is our greatest enemy. He will surely kill you, Rungnir," other Giants cried. "Then he will kill all of us and destroy Jotenheim. You have brought disaster upon us! Not even a Giant can resist Thor with his mighty thunder and his deadly hammer, Miolnir!"

Rungnir, the Giant of the Mountains, looked very ashamed of himself. His fellow Giants at Jotenheim were right to be angry with him. If only he had not gone to Valhalla, the home of Odin, Thor and the Viking gods. If only he had not drunk so much mead when he was there.

'But I am not to blame,' thought Rungnir, as his fellow Giants shouted at him. 'I didn't force my way into Valhalla. Odin, the chief of the gods, invited me in . . . and the mead of the gods did taste wonderful!'

The mead, however, had made Rungnir very drunk, and he started talking very stupidly. "I like this place!" Rungnir cried, looking round the splendid hall in Valhalla, which was lined with shining golden shields. "I will take it back with me to Jotenheim. We Giants are big fellows, as big as mountains. We could do with more room to live in."

Rungnir thumped his enormous fist on the table and laughed loudly. His stone fist made the table shake violently. The sound echoed all through Valhalla.

"I think I shall also take the beautiful Freya and the golden-haired Sif with me," Rungnir decided. "They can be my slaves. As for the rest of you . . ." The Giant looked around at the other gods and goddesses. "I shall kill you all and the Giants shall become the gods of the Vikings instead!"

Thor, the Viking god of thunder, was not at Valhalla. He was busy making storms over the lands of Scandinavia where the Vikings lived. The noise of the storms was very great. All the same, Thor could hear the strange voice coming out of Valhalla. He hurried home to find out what was going on. When he marched into Valhalla and found Rungnir there he was furious.

"What's this? What is a Giant doing here drinking our mead?" Thor demanded in a terrible voice. "Have you all forgotten that the Giants are our deadliest enemies?"

Thor's eyes were blazing with anger. He was swinging his enormous hammer Miolnir in a very threatening manner.

"Odin invited me here," Rungnir protested, his voice trembling.

"What!" shouted Thor, making the shields along the walls clatter with the noise. "Is this true, Odin?"

"Yes," Odin told Thor firmly. "I am chief of the gods. I invite whoever I like to Valhalla. Greet Rungnir as a guest or you will feel my anger!"

Thor knew Odin was all-powerful and could punish him severely, but he was too angry to care. "Greet a Giant as a guest!" he shouted. "Never! I shall kill him where he sits .

"I have no weapon, Thor!" Rungnir cried. "It is a great dishonour to kill an unarmed opponent."

Despite his fury, Thor knew this was true. "Very well, Giant," he replied. "Arm yourself and we shall fight in single combat. Each of us shall have only a squire to attend us."

Rungnir had to accept Thor's challenge. To refuse would make him seem a coward. But when the other Giants learned that Rungnir was to fight Thor, they were horrified. They realised they must do something to stop disaster coming upon them.

The hall at Jotenheim fell silent as the Giants sat and thought about it. The Giants' brains were made of stone. So they were not very intelligent, and it took a long time before one of them thought of an idea.

"I know what we can do," the Giant suggested. "Let's make the biggest and tallest squire there has ever been for Rungnir!"

The other Giants liked the idea. "Splendid! Splendid!" they cried. "Thor only has Thialfi as his squire, and Thialfi is no bigger than a human's fingernail."

The Giants set to work straight away. With their huge fists, they pulled enormous amounts of clay and rock out of the earth and began to build a colossal creature out of it. It grew bigger and bigger until it stretched nine miles into the air. Its chest measured three miles across. It was so enormous that the gods in Valhalla could see it rising up above the mountain peaks.

"Look at that!" Thialfi said to Thor. "That's Rungnir's squire! And look at me! How tiny I am! What are we going to do, great god of thunder?"

It was a problem, even for the mighty Thor.

"We must call a meeting of the gods," Thor told Thialfi. "Together we must decide what to do."

The gods discussed the problem for many hours. Then, at length, the cunning demon, Loki, thought of a solution.

"This is how we shall defeat the Giants' huge creature . . ." said Loki, and he told the other gods of his plan.

The day of the battle dawned. It was very cloudy. The clouds were so thick they hid the sun. Rungnir arrived on the battlefield carrying his hone – a large stone shaped like a letter 'Y'. The minutes passed. The time for the battle to start went by. But where was Thor? He was nowhere to be seen.

"He is afraid to fight Rungnir," said the Giants, feeling very pleased and excited.

More time went by. In Valhalla, all was quiet. It was as if the gods were all asleep.

Then suddenly, there was a tremendous noise beneath Rungnir's feet. The earth shook and shuddered as the noise became louder and louder, until the stone ears of Rungnir began to hurt. The enormous squire was terrified. He began to sweat with fear.

Across the mountains, Loki was watching from his hiding place. Next to Loki was Tir, the sky god.

"It's working, Tir," whispered Loki excitedly. "Are you ready to play your part in our plan when the time comes?"

"Of course," Tir whispered back.

The thundering inside the earth increased. The ground at Rungnir's feet split open with a terrific tearing noise. A great blaze of fire and lightning leapt out of it and there in the middle was Thor. In his hand there was his mighty hammer, Miolnir.

At this, Rungnir's squire gave a frightful shriek. He was sweating so much that he was almost melting into mud. Rungnir was frightened too, but he managed to fling his great hone at Thor. At the same moment, Thor released Miolnir and the hammer went flying through the air, making straight for Rungnir.

"Now, Tir, now!" the watching Loki cried.

The sky god thrust his hand up into the sky and pushed aside the clouds. As they rolled back, the sun shone hot and brilliant. Its rays beat down upon Rungnir's sweating squire, drying him out in a second. At once, huge cracks appeared all over him and he started falling apart. Great chunks of rock and clay began pouring down upon the Giants. They started to run, but only one or two managed to escape. The rest could not run fast enough. The rocks and clay rained down upon them.

Meanwhile, Thor's hammer and Rungnir's hone were flying towards one another. They collided in mid-air. The hone smashed to tiny pieces, but Miolnir was undamaged. It came crashing down at great speed, striking Rungnir on the forehead. Rungnir shattered into stones that fell in a shower all over the earth.

Thor let out a yell of triumph.

"Loki!" he shouted. "You are the cleverest of all the gods in Valhalla."

Loki came out of his hiding place, smiling.

"I never thought that I, Thor, god of thunder, could be more terrifying than I was already," Thor cried, grinning broadly. "But your idea that I tunnel through the earth has proved me wrong."

That night, the merrymaking in Valhalla went on for many hours. A lot of mead was drunk as the gods celebrated Thor's great victory and Loki's cleverness.

81

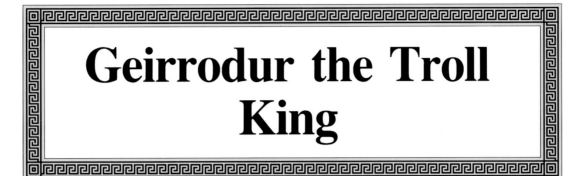

# Geirrodur the Troll King

**G**rid the Giantess was very pleased to see Thor when the thunder god of the Vikings called on her one day. It was a long time since she had seen him. Grid was less pleased, though, when she learned that Thor was on his way to visit Geirrodur, the King of the Trolls. Geirrodur lived in a house made out of a mountain not far from Grid's cottage, and like the Giants who were his cousins, he hated the gods of Valhalla.

"But why visit Geirrodur, Thor?" Grid asked in a worried voice. "Where is your mighty hammer, Miolnir?"

"Miolnir is in Valhalla," said Thor as he sat down to the delicious dinner Grid had cooked for him. "You see, Grid, I have heard that Geirrodur's house is full of marvellous treasures. The walls of his banqueting hall are covered in jewels bright as sunlight. And he has chests full of gold and silver and money . . ." Thor paused to take a huge mouthful of Grid's tasty meat pie. "Geirrodur invited me to come and see it all," Thor went on. "But he was afraid of my hammer Miolnir, so I left it behind."

Then Thor saw Grid's worried face. "What is the matter, Grid?" he asked. "Why are you frowning?"

"Who has told you all this?" Grid asked.

"Loki the demon," Thor replied. "Loki went to Geirrodur's house and saw all the treasures."

"Loki! Oh, no!" Grid's voice sounded alarmed and suspicious. Loki was a very cunning fellow. He was always up to some wicked trick, and Grid guessed this was one of them.

Grid guessed correctly. Geirrodur had caught Loki peeping in through the windows of his mountain house and he had seized and imprisoned him. For a long time Geirrodur had wanted to take revenge on Thor for killing his cousin, Rungnir the Giant. This was his chance to do so.

Geirrodur refused to let Loki go until he promised to persuade Thor to visit his mountain house, and leave the mighty and fearsome Miolnir behind in Valhalla.

"I am sure Loki was lying to you," Grid told Thor. "You know how wicked and mischievous he can be! As for the Trolls, you should never trust them. No, there is some wickedness afoot; some harm will come to you, my dearest Thor." Now Thor was feeling worried. Grid was usually right when she suspected that the enemies of the gods were planning some evil. There was a big problem, though.

"I cannot go back to Valhalla now," Thor protested. "Everyone will think I am a coward. What am I to do?"

Grid went over to the big wooden chest she kept in her dining hall. It contained her most treasured possessions. She opened the lid and pulled some of them out.

"Here," she said, returning to Thor. "Take this Girdle of Might, and this iron

rod. And here are gloves made of iron . . .
They have often protected me against
the Trolls and the Giants. I pray they may
protect you, too!"

Thor was very grateful to Grid. Because
of her warning, he was watching out for
danger as he made his way towards
Geirrodur's mountain house. To get there
he had to cross the River Vimur.

When he reached it, Thor found that the river was not flowing quietly. It was
a raging flood, racing past at tremendous speed.

'Grid's girdle and rod will help me across,' thought Thor. For extra strength,
he fastened the girdle around his waist and as he stepped into the fast-running
waters he rammed the iron rod down into the river bed. The waters pushed
against him with mighty force, but Thor managed to stay upright. Then, in
the middle of the river, Thor suddenly found it was flowing twice as strongly.
Now it was very difficult for him to stay on his feet, even with the iron rod to
steady him.

Just then, Thor saw a female Troll standing on the river bank. She was
watching him with a wicked smile.

"That's Gialp, Geirrodur's daughter!" Thor cried. "Grid has often warned
me against her."

Gialp was holding the banks of the river apart. So, *she* was making the flood
that threatened to drown him!

85

"We'll see about that!" Thor shouted. He picked up a huge boulder from the river bank and threw it at Gialp. With a cry of fright, she jumped aside. The boulder landed in the river with an enormous splash. At once, its waters became as calm as a pond, for the boulder had stopped the river's flow.

When Gialp saw this, she began to run. By the time Thor climbed up the river bank, she was safely inside Geirrodur's mountain house.

"The plan to drown Thor has failed," she told her father, in a disappointed voice. "He is on his way here right now."

"Never mind, daughter," Geirrodur said, with an evil grin. "We have others ways of trapping him! Look!" he said, pointing out of the window. "There go my Trolls to welcome Thor – or so he will think."

As the welcoming Trolls came towards him, Thor was on his guard against danger. Never trust a Troll! Grid had often told Thor that – and she was right! Even so, Thor could not go back now, so he followed the Trolls into the guest house which they had prepared for him.

"Wait here, great Thor," the Trolls asked respectfully. "King Geirrodur is preparing his Great Hall to receive you as you deserve."

Thor sat down on the only chair in the guest house. He was thankful for a rest after his struggle with the river. Thor leaned back. The chair was comfortable. Then suddenly, he felt himself rising upwards. Up and up he went until he was very close to the stone roof of the guest house.

'Grid's iron rod will save me,' Thor thought, and using all his strength he pushed the rod against the roof. Harder and harder he pushed. Then all at once the chair fell and landed on the floor with a loud crash. Thor looked down. The chair had landed on top of Gialp and her sister Greip. They were screaming with pain and fury as they lay trapped beneath.

"Serves you right!" Thor said. "You tried to crush me against the roof, but I have crushed you instead."

King Geirrodur, meanwhile, was warming himself by the fire in his great hall. When he heard shrieks and thumps in the guest house, he thought his daughters had succeeded in crushing Thor. However, when Geirrodur heard the heavy tramp of feet outside and saw the doors flung back, it was not Greip and Gialp who stood there, but Thor. His face was black with rage, as black as a storm.

Terrified, Geirrodur grabbed some fire tongs from behind him. He drew a white-hot bar of iron out of the fire, and flung it at Thor. Quickly the thunder god put on the iron gloves Grid had given him, and caught the bar. "This is yours, Geirrodur!" he roared. And before Geirrodur knew what was happening, Thor had hurled the iron bar back at him.

As it came whizzing across the hall, Geirrodur jumped behind an iron pillar. There was a tremendous crash. Then the pillar and King Geirrodur were lying on the floor of the hall. Both of them had been split in two. The white-hot bar had gone straight through them, and then on through the wall of the house. It did not stop until it buried itself deep in the earth outside.

The Trolls who had been watching all this started yelling in fear and tried to run away. But they could not escape Thor. He strode round the hall, whirling Grid's iron rod from side to side and killing dozens of tiny Trolls with each blow.

Thor was so angry at what had happened in Geirrodur's house that his roars of rage could be heard far away across the mountains in Valhalla.

"Just wait until I get my hands on that demon, Loki!" Thor yelled as he returned to Valhalla in a huge chariot. "He will pay for the lies he told me about Geirrodur's treasure. I will teach him a lesson he will never forget."

The whole of Valhalla trembled as Thor leapt out of his chariot and marched inside shouting, "Loki! Loki! I am coming to get you, Loki!"

Thor looked everywhere, but Loki was nowhere to be found. Loki had in fact, heard Thor returning to Valhalla, and he knew exactly what was going to happen to him if he stayed there. So Loki rushed out of Valhalla and raced towards the mountains. There he hid himself in the furthest passageway in the deepest cave he could find. He crouched there, trembling, as Thor's voice thundered out and made the cave walls shake. Loki stayed in the mountains for a very long time before he dared even to peep outside the cave. It was even longer before he dared to think about returning to Valhalla.

# Siegfried the Dragon Slayer

Siegfried held the point of his sword under Kuperan's chin. He turned it a little, so that the point pricked Kuperan's throat. Kuperan, the King of the Giants, gasped when he felt it.

Siegfried looked menacing. "Are you going to unlock the enchanted cave?" he demanded. "Or am I going to kill you? Choose, Kuperan."

There was no real choice. Kuperan had no wish to die, and certainly not with Euglein, King of the Dwarfs, looking on.

The dwarfs and giants hated each other. Now that Kuperan was at Seigfried's mercy, the Dwarf King was grinning all over his ugly face.

"Let me get up and I'll get the key to the cave," Kuperan growled at Siegfried.

Siegfried took his sword away. Scowling, Kuperan got to his feet.

"The shame of it! The shame of it!" he muttered to himself. "If I don't get my revenge, the dwarfs will laugh at me for ever."

The facts were indeed shameful for Kuperan. The key he held was the only key to the enchanted cave, where the dragon Fafnir guarded the most splendid treasure on Earth. Fafnir was an enormous creature. Once he had been a blacksmith. He was turned into a dragon after he killed his father, Reidmar, and took the treasure from him.

The crystal, gold, silver, jewels and other treasure had been made by the dwarfs. If Kuperan let Siegfried and Euglein into the cave, the dwarfs would get the treasure back. That was the last thing Kuperan wanted. So he refused to give Siegfried the key.

Things had gone badly wrong, however. Siegfried was far stronger than Kuperan imagined. When they fought, Kuperan lost. Now Seigfried was forcing the Giant King to do what he wanted. It did not make Kuperan feel any better to know that Siegfried, son of King Siegmund of the Rhine, was already famous as a powerful warrior and a great dragon slayer. The King of the Giants did not want to be conquered by anyone!

'How can I get my revenge?' Kuperan thought, as he reluctantly took the key to the cave from its hiding place. 'Prince Siegfried may be a great warrior, but he is human and all humans have some weakness.'

Then Kuperan remembered. When Siegfried killed his first dragon, he ate the dragon's flesh. The dragon's thick, scaly horn had grown all over his body. It was like a suit of armour. However, there was one spot between Siegfried's shoulders where a leaf had fallen, and that spot was not covered in horn.

'That is where I shall strike Siegfried when I get the chance,' Kuperan decided, as he led the Prince and Euglein towards the enchanted cave.

Siegfried followed Kuperan warily. He did not trust the Giant King. Euglein stayed close to Siegfried all the way, and while they walked along, the Dwarf King told the Prince more about the treasure in the cave.

"We dwarfs have placed a curse on it," Euglein said. "Whoever possesses the treasure and keeps it from us shall die! But there is one great problem . . ."

"What is that?" Siegfried asked.

"Fafnir, who has the treasure, can only be killed with the magic sword he himself used to kill his father, Reidmar," replied Euglein. "And that sword is hidden away somewhere in the cave. I don't know where it is."

When he heard this, Kuperan turned round. At once, Siegfried pointed his sword at him in case Kuperan attacked. But Kuperan smiled and held up his hands to show that he meant no harm.

"I know where the magic sword is, Prince Siegfried," the giant said. "As you have spared my life, I will show you its hiding place."

Siegfried was pleased to hear this. "Good!" he cried. "Then I can kill Fafnir."

Kuperan chuckled to himself. 'Oh, no you won't, young Siegfried,' he thought. 'I shall kill you first, and I know precisely how I am going to do it.'

At last, they reached the cave. It was hidden behind a waterfall. Kuperan opened the door with his key. Behind the door lay a long, winding passage. There was a strange light glowing there. As Kuperan led Siegfried and Euglein along it, the light became brighter and brighter. Suddenly, they entered a huge hall and Siegfried saw that the light had come from the gold covering its wall and the large jewels that studded it.

"No wonder this is called the most splendid treasure in the world!" breathed Siegfried, as he looked about him in wonder.

Suddenly, there was a deep rumbling not far away. The floor of the cave trembled. The rumbling became a roar, and Siegfried heard a swishing, howling sound. Greatly frightened, Euglein jumped behind a nearby rock and hid himself.

"It's Fafnir!" Kuperan whispered. "The dragon – he's coming and he's breathing fire and flames. Quick, Prince Siegfried, get the magic sword!"

Kuperan hurried across the room and drew back a thick curtain that hung on one side. There, behind it, was a sword. It was embedded in a large stone.

"This is the magic sword that can kill Fafnir, if you can get it out of the stone," Kuperan told Siegfried.

Siegfried rushed over to the sword and grasped the hilt. He began pulling and heaving at it but the sword was difficult to move.

All at once, there was a sharp cry. "Prince Siegfried! Look out!" It was Euglein. Siegfried turned his head and saw the tiny Dwarf King fling himself across the hall and collide with Kuperan's hand. Kuperan shouted in surprise as the dagger in his hand was knocked to the floor. He had been about to plunge the dagger into the unprotected spot on Siegfried's back. Kuperan reached down and snatched up the dagger, but Siegfried was too quick for him. With one last terrific effort, he pulled the sword out of the stone, and plunged it into Kuperan. At once Kuperan fell to the floor, dead.

"A sword that can kill a dragon can also kill a traitor!" Siegfried cried angrily.

Now the roaring was getting louder and louder. Suddenly, Euglein shrieked, "He's here! Fafnir's here!" The Dwarf King leapt back into his hiding place and ducked down out of sight.

The next moment the hall became tremendously hot and Fafnir appeared. He was indeed a colossal creature, covered all over in thick scales. With each deafening roar, a mass of flames leapt out of his mouth. The heat was so terrific that Siegfried's shield became red hot.

Fafnir was coming straight towards Siegfried. His eyes were like enormous pools of fire and there was a ferocious look in them.

Siegfried looked for somewhere to shelter. He saw a passageway between the rocks that was too small for Fafnir to follow and darted into it. While Fafnir roared and stamped outside, Siegfried picked up a large rock. He crept to the entrance of the passageway and flung the stone at Fafnir with all his strength. Siegfried's aim was good. The rock flew into Fafnir's mouth and stuck in his throat.

At once, the flames stopped coming out of Fafnir's throat. Seeing this, Siegfried rushed forward and began to slash at the dragon's scales with the magic sword. To his horror, he found that even this wonderful weapon could not pierce the thick scales.

Then a small voice sounded from the other side of the cave.

"Fafnir! Fafnir! Over here, Fafnir!" It was Euglein's voice.

The dragon looked round to see who had spoken. As he did so, Siegfried saw a space between his thick scales. He lunged forward and plunged the magic sword into the gap. It sank right in. Siegfried pulled it out, ready to strike Fafnir again, but he was driven back by an enormous blaze of fire which poured out of the wound. Fafnir went wild with pain, and began thrashing about with his huge tail. Even so, Siegfried leapt forward again and once more plunged the magic sword between two of Fafnir's scales. This time it went directly into his heart. A fearful gurgling noise came out of the dragon's throat and he collapsed to the floor with a thunderous crash. The last of the flames flickered out and the light in his fearsome eyes grew dark. Fafnir was dead.

King Euglein came dancing out from his hiding place, laughing with delight. He jumped up and embraced Siegfried.

"At last, at last!" Euglein cried. "The treasure the dwarfs created belongs to the dwarfs again."

As a reward, Euglein gave Siegfried one of the most beautiful jewels in the enchanted cave. Siegfried wore it on his shield, so that his enemies would know he was the mighty Prince of the Rhine who in one day killed the King of the Giants and the King of Dragons.

94

# Beowulf

**B**eowulf and his fourteen horsemen rode swiftly towards the palace of King Hrothgar of Denmark. It was already getting dark. They must hurry. They must reach the palace before the monster Grendel got there. It was time someone stopped the dreadful activities of this monster and put an end to the terror he was causing. Every night Grendel invaded Hrothgar's feasting hall, Heorot, and carried off one of his warriors. These Danish warriors were once the greatest and bravest in northern Europe. Now they were afraid to stay at Heorot after dark.

Beowulf, a nobleman of the Geatas people of Sweden, was very angry when he heard of this.

"The Danes are our brothers!" he declared. "We cannot let the world laugh at them and call them cowards. We must kill Grendel and free the Danes from his tyranny. Who will come with me?"

Fourteen Geatas warriors came forward at once and offered to accompany Beowulf. They sailed for Denmark that night.

By the following evening, they were riding full speed along the track that led to King Hrothgar's palace. They galloped into the palace courtyard just as the last rays of the sun were fading from the sky.

Quickly, Beowulf and his men dismounted and hurried inside the palace. King Hrothgar was waiting for them.

"You are the most welcome of guests, Beowulf!" he said warmly. "Now at last we can be rid of the terrible Grendel!"

Beowulf came quickly to the point. "Is everything ready as I asked?" he wanted to know.

Hrothgar nodded and led him into the hall of Heorot, where the tables were laid for a great feast. A fire burned warmly in the centre of the hall. A sheep was turning on the spit set up over the fire.

Beowulf looked round the hall. "It is very well done," he said. "Leave Heorot in my charge tonight, Your Majesty, and I promise that tomorrow night you may hold a great feast of celebration. For by tomorrow night Grendel will be dead!"

Soon afterwards, sounds of great feasting and merrymaking were heard. Beowulf and his fourteen men were enjoying themselves in the hall of Heorot.

"This is food fit for kings!" they shouted. "This is wine fit for the gods! More, bring us more!"

Though they sounded very drunk and carefree, they were actually very much on the alert. All of them were closely watching the door where Grendel would soon appear.

"You all know what you have to do," Beowulf had told them. "The noise we make will draw Grendel to the hall, and then we will strike."

The noise certainly did draw Grendel towards Heorot. While Beowulf and his warriors were feasting, Grendel was approaching.

When he smelled the delicious odours of the meat, and saw the bright light of the fire, he licked his lips.

"There are dozens of them in there!" Grendel chuckled. "I shall have a great feast tonight – the dinner AND the men who eat it!"

Suddenly, Beowulf and his men saw a huge, dark shape filling the doorway. Grendel had arrived. As they expected, he was a mighty monster with broad shoulders and thick, strong arms. Grendel came clumping into the hall, each footfall making the whole place shake.

"Let him get further in," Beowulf whispered. He was watching Grendel closely. Then he yelled, "Now! Get him now!"

Beowulf's men snatched up their swords and, as their leader had instructed them, they all rushed towards Grendel. Before the monster could move, he was surrounded by a ring of swords pointing directly at him.

"No feast for you tonight, Grendel!" Beowulf shouted. "Your nights of feasting are over!"

Grendel became terrified. He hit out with both fists and knocked five or six of Beowulf's men to the floor. When the others tried to attack him, Grendel gave a great kick with his foot and their swords flew out of their hands and went spinning across the hall. The hall was filled with the sound of groans from Beowulf's men as they lay on the floor, bruised and aching.

Grendel was now very angry. He looked about him, growling. He saw one of the men trying to get up. Grendel pounced on him and snatched him up, struggling and yelling. Before anyone could move to stop him, Grendel opened his mouth and stuffed his victim into it. Grendel's great teeth crushed him to death. It was a horrible sight.

Beowulf suddenly leapt up and flung himself at Grendel. Beowulf's hands grasped Grendel's wrist and his fingers closed round as if they were locked into place.

Grendel pulled and struggled and tried to shake Beowulf off. Beowulf refused to let go. With one last terrific effort Grendel heaved himself back, hoping to escape Beowulf's grasp in one go. Instead, there was a ghastly tearing sound. Beowulf tumbled to the floor and Grendel staggered towards the doorway moaning and crying and clutching his shoulder. Beowulf stared in amazement. No wonder! For Beowulf still had his hands locked around Grendel's wrist.

"I've pulled his arm off!" Beowulf gasped.

Grendel, meanwhile, had disappeared through the doorway. His moans and cries could be heard outside as he stumbled away.

"After him!" cried Beowulf. "Quickly!"

Beowulf's men were too bruised and dazed to get to their feet quickly. By the time they set off after Grendel, the monster had disappeared from sight.

Then suddenly, one of Beowulf's men shouted, "Look! Here's Grendel's blood!"

"Here's some more!" said another. "The monster has left a trail of blood."

By the light of the moon, Beowulf and his men followed the trail of blood along the path that led away from Hrothgar's palace. It led to the edge of a small lake.

"Look at the water!" Beowulf told them. "It's red!"

The water of the lake was a deep dark red. It was as if there were more blood than water in it.

"Grendel has drowned!" Beowulf said. "He must have fallen into the lake and could not climb out again."

"We have destroyed the monster! Our dead comrade is avenged! Let us get back to Heorot and tell King Hrothgar the news."

Beowulf and his men were right to think that Grendel was dead. They were wrong, though, to think that he had drowned in the lake.

As he stumbled away from Heorot, Grendel knew he was dying. All he wanted to do was reach his home in the depths of the lake. He had succeeded. Once inside, he collapsed and as his mother wept over him, Grendel died.

"They shall pay for this!" his mother wailed. "I shall kill them one at a time, so that the rest can live in fear and terror, awaiting my return!"

When King Hrothgar heard that Grendel was dead and would trouble him no more, he ordered a splendid feast of celebration to be held the following night. It was certainly a great occasion. Jugglers and tumblers and musicians came to entertain the guests. Poets recited verses praising Beowulf and his companions. All the servants were kept busy filling and refilling the drinking horns with wine so that King Hrothgar and his guests could drink the health of the heroes who had killed the terrible Grendel.

"How can I thank you, Beowulf!" he cried. "Half my kingdom – or all of it – could not be enough to show how grateful I am."

Just then, a frightening sound reached the ears of everyone at the feast. It was a great, deep, angry roar.

"It sounds like . . . but it can't be . . . " King Hrothgar gasped fearfully. "It can't be Grendel! You told me he was dead!"

Beowulf was just as surprised as the King. "Grendel is dead!" he declared. "He could not have lived long after I tore off his arm."

The roaring reached their ears again. It came nearer and nearer. Then, without warning, a huge giantess came rushing through the doorway. It was Grendel's mother.

"Which of you killed my son? I will be avenged!" She looked round the hall, snarling. Some of the people at the tables turned pale with fear and scrambled from their seats, rushing for the doors.

"I will start with the one who tore off his arm!" Grendel's mother cried, shaking her fists with fury. "Who was it? Show yourself!"

Beowulf jumped to his feet. "It was I!" he declared. "It was a deed well done."

"This too is a deed well done!" Grendel's mother retorted, and she leapt at Beowulf, seized him by the arm and started to drag him across the floor. Beowulf struggled, but her grip was too strong. As King Hrothgar and his guests watched in horror, Grendel's mother dragged Beowulf through the doorway and disappeared.

"After them!" the King cried. "After them and rescue Beowulf!" But everyone, including Beowulf's own men, was too startled and too horrified to move.

Beowulf felt the hard ground scratching and bruising him as Grendel's mother pulled him along the path. She was muttering and moaning to herself as she went. From what she said, Beowulf realised she was taking him to her home beneath the lake.

Beowulf thought quickly. He had his sword and fortunately Grendel's mother was not dragging him by his sword arm. He could fight for his life – when he got the chance!

Grendel's mother reached the lake and keeping a firm grip on Beowulf's arm, plunged into the water. When she reached her home, she pulled Beowulf through the door and into the room where Grendel lay dead.

Grendel's mother began to weep and wail. "See! See what you have done!" she cried, pointing to Grendel's body and the torn shoulder where his arm had once been.

For onc momcnt, Bcowulf felt pity for the grief-stricken mother, monster though she was. The moment passed quickly, though. Grendel's mother soon turned angry and flung Beowulf roughly into a corner.

"Wait there!" she growled. "You can watch as I prepare the vessels in which I will boil you alive!"

She turned her back on Beowulf and reached up for a huge cauldron which stood on a shelf above the fire. This was just the chance Beowulf had been waiting for. He jumped up, drew his sword and rushed towards Grendel's mother.

She heard him, however, and turned round just as Beowulf was halfway across the room. With a yell of fury, Grendel's mother flung the cauldron at him. Beowulf ducked. The cauldron flew over his head and clattered across the floor. Then Grendel's mother kicked out and knocked Beowulf's sword from his hand.

She let out a shout of triumph and lunged towards Beowulf, her great hands open, ready to grasp him. But Beowulf stepped nimbly out of the way. Grendel's mother stumbled and crashed face downwards on to the floor. Then Beowulf saw a huge sword leaning against the wall in one corner.

'Grendel's sword!' he thought, as he darted across and took hold of its hilt. 'Big enough, anyway to kill a giantess.'

The sword was very, very heavy, but the danger he was facing gave Beowulf the extra strength he needed. Grendel's mother was just raising herself off the floor when Beowulf swung the sword round in a mighty sweeping movement. The blade struck straight through her neck, slicing off her head. The force of the blow was so great that the sword broke and Beowulf found himself with just the hilt of the sword in his hand.

Beowulf arrived back at Heorot to find his companions sitting sadly at the tables, where he had left them. They were certain that Beowulf was dead. They started up in surprise when they heard his voice.

"You may prepare for another celebration, Your Majesty," said Beowulf as he walked into the hall.

"You have fought and struggled hard," said King Hrothgar, looking at Beowulf's torn clothes and dirty, mud-stained face.

"No matter," Beowulf replied. "Grendel is dead and I bring you gifts that will gladden Your Majesty's heart."

Proudly, Beowulf laid the broken sword hilt and the head of Grendel's mother on the table before the King.

"This is a great day, Beowulf!" King Hrothgar declared. "There shall indeed be a great feast to celebrate it. For you came here to Heorot to kill one monster – but instead you have killed two!"

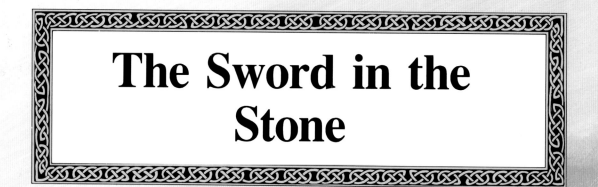

# The Sword in the Stone

No one knew how the square slab of marble-stone came to be in the churchyard. One moment, there was nothing there but empty ground. The next moment, or so it seemed, the huge slab simply appeared. And what a stone it was! It looked as if it had been hewn from the side of a mountain. On top of it stood a great iron anvil, and buried deep in the anvil was the long, sharp, shining steel blade of a sword.

It was Christmas day, and the knights of King Uther Pendragon had come to pray in the church. For this one day, they seemed willing to set aside their constant quarrelling over which of them should be King of Britain. The rivalry had been going on ever since King Uther died, with no son to succeed him. It was violent rivalry. Each knight was willing to kill all the others in order to possess the throne.

104

Merlin the Magician sighed as he looked round at the brutish faces of the knights in the church. It was tragic that men like these should be the leaders of the Britons, for they were more interested in their own ambitions than in the welfare of their nation. While Uther's knights were squabbling, Britain was in a terrible plight. Year by year, fierce Anglo-Saxon invaders were conquering more and more of the land. If the Britons were to stop them, they must have a King – a King acknowledged by all as their true and only rightful ruler. That was the purpose of the sword in the stone. It was the only means by which Merlin could show the people who their King really was.

When the knights left the church, they spotted the stone straight away. At once, they crowded round it and ran their fingers over the hard surface of the stone. They looked with amazement and admiration at the mighty steel sword. It was the sort of sword that could kill all rivals, and there was not a man there who did not long to own it.

Then one of the knights saw the words carved in golden lettering along the side of the stone. They read: 'Whoso pulleth out this sword from this stone and anvil is the true-born King of all Britain.'

As soon as they saw this message, the knights rushed forward, only too eager to pull the sword out of the anvil. They pushed and shoved and shouted, demanding to be the first.

Eventually, one knight barged in front and grasped the hilt. He pulled. The sword did not move. He heaved and hauled, using all his strength. It would not budge. Angry and disappointed, the knight gave up. He was followed by another and another, all of them straining to get the sword out until they turned blue in the face with the effort. The sword did not move a single centimetre.

The knights were furious. Merlin was standing nearby, watching them with that mysterious smile of his. The knights shook their fists at him.

105

"This is one of your tricks, Merlin!" they raged. "You've put a spell on this sword."

"No trick, Sir Knight," Merlin replied quietly. "It simply means that none of you is the true-born King of Britain."

"Where is he, then?" growled one of the knights, a large man with a nasty look on his face. "If I ever get my hands on him, I'll fight him for the throne – true-born King or not!"

"You may get your chance, if you dare to take it," Merlin told him. "There will be a great tournament here on New Year's Day. Knights have been summoned from near and far to joust and fight with swords – and all will try to draw the sword from this stone. We shall see if any can do so!"

In the week between Christmas Day and New Year, the roads were filled with splendid processions of knights, all mounted on great strong horses, and followed by their squires and servants. They were heading towards the great tournament. All hoped to draw the sword from the stone and so be proclaimed King of Britain.

Among the knights was Sir Ector and his son Sir Kay, and with them came Sir Ector's younger son, Arthur. Arthur was only sixteen, too young to be a knight. He could not take part in the jousting, but he could assist his father and brother and look after their weapons and their horses.

By the time New Year's Day dawned, the field where the tournament was to be held was crowded with bell-shaped tents of brilliant colours. From the top of each one fluttered the flag of the knight who owned it. Each flag had its own special pattern and design. Arthur sat by the side of the field and looked round excitedly. He was always happiest when he was among fine horses and brave fighting men, and he loved the noise and bustle and thrills of the tournament.

Suddenly, Arthur saw his brother Sir Kay riding towards him. Sir Kay seemed to be in a great hurry.

"I've left my second sword behind at our lodgings," he told Arthur. "How stupid of me. How could I have forgotten it? Will you run and get it for me?"

Arthur scrambled quickly to his feet. He loved and admired his elder brother and liked doing things for him.

"Of course I will," Arthur replied. He ran off to the house nearby where he, his brother and his father were staying while the tournament lasted. Arthur soon reached the door of the house, but found, to his dismay, that it was locked. He banged on the door and shouted, but no one was there.

'Everyone must be at the tournament,' thought Arthur. 'What shall I do? My brother Kay must have his sword.'

Suddenly Arthur remembered the sword in the stone. It was there, in the churchyard, for none of the knights had succeeded in drawing it out.

Quickly, Arthur ran to the churchyard, clambered up on to the great stone, and pulled the sword out of the anvil. It was very beautiful. Arthur admired its fine, broad blade and the way it shone in the winter sunshine.

'Sir Kay will be very pleased with this,' Arthur thought, turning the blade from side to side so that it sparkled in the light.

107

At that moment, Arthur had forgotten all about the message carved on the side of the stone. But Sir Kay and Sir Ector had not forgotten. When they saw Arthur coming towards them waving the great sword to show he had done as Sir Kay had asked, they gasped with astonishment.

"Here, brother Kay," Arthur panted, somewhat out of breath with all the running about he had done. "Here is a fine sword for you . . . "

"Where did you get this?" Sir Ector asked Arthur.

"From the churchyard – it was sticking in the anvil," Arthur explained, suddenly worried to see the serious expression on his father's face. "Have I done wrong, Father?" he asked anxiously.

Sir Ector shook his head and put a hand on his young son's shoulder. His hand, Arthur noticed, was trembling.

"No, you have not done wrong, Arthur," Sir Ector said. "But let us go to the churchyard and see you take the sword from the stone again."

"Put the sword back in the stone, Arthur," Sir Ector commanded him, when they reached the churchyard. The sword slid into the anvil smoothly and easily.

Sir Ector beckoned to Sir Kay. "Try to take it out," he told him. Sir Kay grasped the hilt and pulled. He pulled again. He heaved at it a third time. The sword seemed firmly stuck.

"What is the matter, brother Kay?" Arthur asked. "Why can't you move the sword? Look – it's easy!" He reached up, grasped the sword hilt and slid the blade out of the anvil with one swift movement.

Suddenly, to Arthur's amazement, his father and brother knelt on the ground before him. They were bowing their heads to him in reverence.

"What are you doing?" Arthur cried. "Why do you kneel to me?"

"Because you are the true-born King of all Britain," Sir Ector said. "I am honoured to pledge you my allegiance and to serve you."

108

Arthur was dumbfounded. "Me? A King?" he gasped. "There must be some mistake!"

"No, Arthur," said a voice behind him. "There is no mistake."

It was Merlin. He had been watching everything from the shadow of the church door. Now the magician came forward, holding a magnificent gold scabbard and belt.

"Take this, Arthur," Merlin said. "It is yours. I have waited many years to give it to you, for I have known ever since you were born that you, and no other, are the true-born King of Britain!"

Arthur was unable to speak. He simply gazed wonderstruck at the shining gold scabbard. He turned it over and over in his hands. Merlin watched him and for a moment felt sad that such a young boy should be burdened with so awesome a destiny. As King of Britain, Merlin knew that Arthur would not find it easy to bring peace to his people after so many years of rivalry and fighting. Also the Anglo Saxons, whom Arthur would have to fight, were not easy foes to overcome. But all that lay in the future. Now was the time for celebrations.

"Come!" said Merlin. "We must tell the people that their King has made himself known at last. They have waited a long time to hear this glad news."

# Sir Gawain and the Green Knight

**S**uddenly, there was a mighty crash and a bang, followed by the thundering of iron hooves on a stone floor. Then the great doors of the banqueting hall at Camelot Castle burst open. A huge man came galloping in on an enormous horse. He drew to a halt in the middle of the room.

Startled, King Arthur and his Knights jumped up from their seats at the Round Table. They stared, speechless, at the strange intruder. He was green from head to foot. His jerkin and cloak were green, his spurs were green, his hair and beard and skin were green. Even his horse was green.

"Which of you is the leader of this gathering?" the intruder boomed.

King Arthur stepped forward. "Who wishes to speak with him?" he demanded proudly.

"I am the mighty Green Knight of the North!" came the reply. "I have come to Camelot to see for myself whether all I have heard of this place is true."

"And what have you heard?" King Arthur wanted to know.

"That this castle is the home of the bravest knights and the mightiest and most gracious King," the Green Knight replied. He looked round rather disdainfully. "But now I am here, it seems that you are nothing but weaklings and beardless youths. I could kill every one of you with one stroke of my axe."

At this, several Knights jumped up and drew their swords, ready to kill this impudent intruder. Arthur put up his hand to restrain them. He turned to the Green Knight. "You have made a great boast, sir," said the King. "You must prove it. You have spoken disdainfully of my Knights. For that, they are honour bound to challenge you."

The Green Knight threw back his great head and laughed loudly. "There is no Knight of yours who would dare take up my challenge," he boasted.

"I will do so, whatever it may be!" said the young, impetuous Sir Gawain. He was one of the most daring of Arthur's Knights. "What is your challenge?" Sir Gawain cried. "Speak!"

The Green Knight leaned over and took from the side of his saddle a huge green axe. Its blade was at least twice the length of a man's hand and its finely sharpened edge winked and sparkled in the torchlight.

"I challenge you to exchange blow for blow with me with this great axe of mine," said the Green Knight. "I will kneel here on the floor and receive the first blow. Only remember this," the Knight continued menacingly, "you must swear on your honour to meet me next Christmastide and unarmed, receive the second blow from me."

At this, there was a gasp from all round the banqueting hall. The Green Knight must be a madman! That axe of his could slice through the head of an ox. Everyone, including Sir Gawain, was staring at the Green Knight in amazement and disbelief. The Green Knight mistook their moment of silence for fear. He laughed scornfully.

"As I thought," he said. "You are cowards every one – my challenge is too great for you!"

Sir Gawain's face turned red with fury. "This fellow's insults are more than I can bear," he cried. "I accept your challenge."

The Green Knight gave a grim smile as he swung his leg over the saddle and dropped down to the floor. He was a giant – half as tall again as Sir Gawain. All the same, Sir Gawain was undeterred.

"Give me the axe," he demanded. Gawain took the axe, and tested it by swinging it to and fro a few times. "I am ready," Sir Gawain said. "Are you prepared for the first blow, Sir Knight?"

The Green Knight knelt down on the floor, drew his long hair aside so that his neck was exposed and bent his head forward.

"Strike now!" he boomed.

"Gladly," cried Sir Gawain and with one great swing of the axe he brought it swishing round towards the Green Knight's neck. The blade went straight through and the Green Knight's head toppled off and rolled on to the floor.

Sir Gawain turned pale with horror, but the Green Knight chuckled. "I am not harmed!" he said. His body rose up, stepped across to where his head lay and grasped it by the hair. Then the Green Knight leapt back on his horse.

"Remember your oath, Sir Knight," said the Green Knight. "Seek me out at my castle in the North next Christmastide."

With that, the Green Knight wheeled his horse about and with a great clattering and clanging of hooves galloped out as noisily as he had come.

The following December, Sir Gawain set out from Camelot to seek the castle of the Green Knight. The way there was long and hard, and the weather raw and icy cold. Many times when snow blizzards were blowing all around him and the wind seemed to slice into his very bones, he wished he was back in Camelot.

It was only a passing thought, though. Sir Gawain fully intended to keep his strange bargain with the Green Knight. It was, however, curious that Sir Gawain should meet so many people on the road who tried to divert him from his purpose.

112

First, there was the nobleman who stopped him along the road and offered to entertain him at his castle nearby.

"There are great fires there to warm you," the nobleman promised. "And a great feast, with as much wine as you can drink. After the feast, you may rest in a bed covered in soft feathers."

Sir Gawain thanked the nobleman, but refused his offer. "No, kind sir," he told him. "I am bound by my oath to meet the Green Knight at his castle."

Sir Gawain rode on, freezing cold and very hungry. He met a huntsman next. The huntsman hailed him and, like the nobleman, seemed very hospitable and generous.

"The castle of the Green Knight is far away, Sir Gawain," the huntsman told him. "Surely you would rather come hunting with me and my friends? It is warm, exciting sport and there are plenty of deer and wild pigs hereabouts. Afterwards, we can have a great feast. What say you, Sir?"

Again, Sir Gawain refused. "I thank you, Sir. Your offer is kind," he replied. "But I am bound by my oath to meet the Green Knight."

Next, a knight appeared on the road, clad in full armour and obviously on his way to a tournament. The knight offered to take Sir Gawain with him so that they could test their fighting skills against each other and afterwards feast and talk round a roaring fire. Once again, Gawain refused and journeyed on towards the castle of the Green Knight.

At long last, the castle came in sight. It was, of course, all green. Its high towers and great battlements made beautiful patterns against the winter sky. Sir Gawain rode into the courtyard as the sky was beginning to grow dark. It was Christmas Eve.

The Green Knight was there, waiting for him. His head was back on his shoulders again, with no sign of the axe-stroke which had severed his neck a year ago.

"Welcome," cried the Green Knight, grinning gleefully at Sir Gawain. "Let us to our business straight away. I have been impatient this last year, waiting for this moment."

The Green Knight was just as terrible as Sir Gawain remembered him, and his great green axe looked as mighty and as sharp as before. Silently, Sir Gawain murmured his prayers as he followed the Green Knight into the castle.

They reached the hall and the Green Knight pointed to a spot on the stone floor. "Kneel there, Sir Gawain," he instructed. "Here is where I answer the blow you gave me last Christmastide."

With one last prayer, Sir Gawain knelt down, pushed his hair aside and bent his head forward.

"Make ready to strike," Sir Gawain told the Green Knight in a firm, clear voice. "I am a Knight of the Round Table and I shall keep my vow to you, even if it costs me my life. Unlike you, I cannot replace my head when it falls to your axe. Come, Sir, strike!"

The Green Knight lifted up the axe and swung it swiftly towards Sir Gawain's neck.

Sir Gawain felt the rush of air it made. But the blade did not touch him.
The Knight stopped it a finger's breadth away from Sir Gawain's neck. Sir
Gawain looked up, curious and startled.

"You are playing games with me!" he accused the Green Knight. "It is not
chivalrous to act so!"

Then he noticed that the Green Knight was smiling at him, not disdainfully as
he had seen him smile before, but with a friendly look on his face. The Knight
placed his great hand under Sir Gawain's elbow and raised him to his feet.

"No, I am playing no game – only testing your courage and honour," said
the Green Knight quietly. "You did not flinch from my axe-blade just now.
That took great courage. When I set all manner of temptations on the road
between here and Camelot to divert you from your purpose, you refused all of
them, even though you were cold and tired and hungry. That takes a truly
honourable spirit."

Sir Gawain gasped. "So it was you!" he cried. "Why, Sir, you tempted me
with the sweetest comforts any knight could ask for!"

"Then you shall enjoy them all now," the Green Knight smiled. "I have
achieved my task, set me by Merlin, to make sure that King Arthur and
his Knights remain the bravest and most honourable Knights in Britain. You
have certainly proved that they are. Now, Sir Gawain, we shall feast, we shall
hunt and tomorrow there is a tournament, here at my castle. And tonight, you
may sleep in comfort. You have well deserved it."

# Rodrigo of Spain

**K**ing Rodrigo of Spain was very suspicious. He had never heard anything as ridiculous as the story the two strange old men had come to tell him. They were an odd sight, clad in long white robes, with stars and moons embroidered all over them. They looked like magicians or sorcerers. From their girdles, there hung bunches of rusty old keys. These, they said, were the keys to padlocks which Spanish kings had fixed to the door of the Enchanted Tower in past years.

According to the two old men, each king had woven a spell around his padlocks, to keep the Muslims from invading Christian Spain. Now the two old men wanted King Rodrigo to do the same.

'Enchanted Tower, magic spells, padlocks . . .' King Rodrigo thought. 'I don't believe a word of it!'

However, the Tower did sound interesting. It was made of marble and the rich jewel, jasper. With all that wealth outside, who knew what treasure lay inside?

"Very well," said Rodrigo. "Take me to the Tower. But I will not fix a padlock until I have entered it and seen what is inside."

At this, the two old men started wailing and wringing their hands.

"No, no, Your Majesty!" they cried in great anxiety. "No one must enter the Tower! It is forbidden. If you enter the Tower, the Muslims will be sure to invade Spain. We beg you, Your Majesty, we entreat you, do not go into the Tower!"

"Nonsense, babbling nonsense!" Rodrigo replied. He rose from his throne and walked across to the two old men. He poked one of them roughly in the ribs.

"I know what you are doing!" Rodrigo snarled at him. "You have hidden treasure in the Tower, and you want me to put another lock on it so that it will be even safer than it is now."

The old men raised their hands in horror.

"No, no! It's not true! We have never been inside the Tower. We told you – disaster awaits if anyone enters the Tower, even you, Your Majesty."

Rodrigo looked very angry. "You are lying! I'll hear no more of this nonsense. You will take me to the Tower and you will unlock it for me. I will see what is inside, and if I find you have been keeping treasure from me, both of you shall die!"

Immediately, Rodrigo ordered horses to be saddled and together with the old men and two of his knights, he galloped out of his palace and rode swiftly to the Tower.

117

It was beautiful. Tall and straight, with brightly shining walls, covered in red, yellow and brown jasper. Rodrigo gazed at it, entranced. He rode round the Tower several times, wondering at its beauty and more sure than ever that lying inside he would find fabulous wealth in gold, silver and jewels.

Rodrigo made the old men dismount from their horses. Both of them were shaking with fear.

"Unlock the Tower!" Rodrigo ordered them. "Stop that noise!" he growled as the two old men broke into loud wailing cries.

Once more, Rodrigo commanded them to be silent, but they went on crying and moaning and wringing their hands.

Rodrigo was becoming impatient. These two old fools were so terrified, they might take a month to undo all those padlocks. There were at least a dozen of them. Rodrigo turned to his two knights. "Break it open!" he commanded. "Your axes and swords should be able to break those padlocks."

It was hard work. Half an hour passed before one of the knights finally managed to break the last chain across the door of the Tower. It fell away and Rodrigo hurried forward to turn the handle and open the door.

Slowly, the door creaked inwards. It was very dark inside the Tower, and for a moment, even Rodrigo felt afraid. However, with the thought of the treasure inside, his fear vanished and he marched through the doorway and into the entrance hall of the Tower.

For a moment, Rodrigo could see nothing. Then, as his eyes grew accustomed to the dim light, he saw gold and silver glittering on a great marble table in the centre of the hall. He gasped. The table was covered with gold and silver coins.

Rodrigo rushed towards the table, followed by his two knights. The two old men remained outside, shaking with anxiety and fear. Rodrigo picked up two handfuls of coins and let them trickle through his fingers. It was a wonderful feeling.

In the centre of the table, stood a marble urn. Rodrigo was sure that more treasure lay inside.

118

Swiftly, he pushed aside the lid of the urn, and plunged in his hand. But instead of jewels or more coins, all Rodrigo could feel was a piece of parchment. He drew it out and, rather mystified, unrolled it.

It was a picture painted in brilliant colours. The picture showed a line of horsemen, bearing long spears in their hands. The horsemen were brown-skinned, like the people across the Straits of Gibraltar, in Morocco. Like them, they had long, thick, shaggy hair and from their belts hung strange curved swords like the ones the Muslims used in battle.

"Look, Your Majesty!" said one of the knights. "There is something written below the picture." He began to read and as he did so, his voice started to tremble.

"Behold, when the door of this Tower is forced open by violence and the spell contained in this urn is broken, then the people painted on this picture will invade Spain . . . " The knight faltered, unable to read on for a moment. Then he continued: " . . . then the people painted on this picture will invade Spain, overthrow the throne of her King and conquer the whole country!"

King Rodrigo had turned very pale. He had expected to find treasure, not this dreadful prophecy of doom and disaster. He looked again at the picture and its brown-skinned horsemen. He began to shiver.

Then suddenly, as Rodrigo watched, the picture came to life. The brown-skinned horsemen were galloping, waving their spears in the air . . . Behind them, Rodrigo saw a flag with a star and a crescent on it: the flag of the Muslims! A violent battle was being fought in the picture. Rodrigo recognised the Christian knights of Spain, struggling against the horsemen, and falling from their saddles one by one.

There was one horse in particular which caught Rodrigo's attention. It belonged to the Christian army and it was snow-white in colour. On its back was a saddle decorated with beautiful jewels. The jewels were glittering in the sunshine. Where was the rider? He was nowhere to be seen.

Rodrigo let out a cry of fear. He knew that beautiful snow-white horse. He knew that bejewelled saddle. Frantically, Rodrigo searched the picture for the rider of the snow-white horse, but he could not find him.

Suddenly, Rodrigo realised what that meant, and panic took hold of him. He turned and rushed out of the Tower. As he ran through the doorway, he nearly fell over two bodies lying outside it. They were the bodies of the two old men. They were dead.

Rodrigo did not stop. He leaped on to his horse, and with his knights following close behind, galloped away from the Tower at high speed. As they raced down the hillside, they heard a deafening explosion. They turned, to see the Tower engulfed in blood-red flames and clouds of black smoke. When the smoke cleared, the Tower was gone. In its place was a heap of molten ruins.

For years afterwards, King Rodrigo tried hard to forget the Tower and the dreadful things he saw in the moving picture. In particular, Rodrigo tried to forget the snow-white horse without a rider. To help himself forget, Rodrigo went hunting, or gave great banquets in his palace at Toledo. He made long journeys through his kingdom and held splendid tournaments where his knights fought mock battles against each other.

Nothing helped. Rodrigo could never forget the Tower and the dreadful prophecy he had seen there. In any case, how could Rodrigo forget when every year brought dreadful news from North Africa, across the Mediterranean Sea. Every year, hordes of Muslim warriors advanced westwards along the North African coast. First, Rodrigo heard they were in Libya. Then they were through the Atlas Mountains, and were pouring into Morocco. Finally, Rodrigo received the news he most dreaded to hear. The Muslim fleet was crossing the Straits of Gibraltar and making for the coast of Spain.

At once, King Rodrigo gathered his army of knights, nobles and thousands of foot soldiers. This great army set out to meet the Muslims on a battleground near the River Gaudalete.

As soon as Rodrigo saw the huge Muslim hordes, he knew the battle was lost.

"Brown skins . . . long, shaggy hair . . . those long spears and curved swords," he murmured to himself as he looked at the Muslims. "They are all like the horsemen in the picture . . . the picture was a portent."

He was right. The battle was hard-fought; just as it was in the picture. Yet however hard they fought, the Spanish knights could not overcome the Muslims. One by one they were killed and toppled from their saddles to the ground. Tarik, the Muslim leader, searched for King Rodrigo. He soon found him, for no one had a snow-white horse like the King of Spain. No one had a jewelled saddle like the one on which Rodrigo sat.

Tarik pushed his way through the mass of struggling soldiers and rearing, whinnying horses.

"Fight to the death, Rodrigo!" Tarik cried. Thrusting his sword in front of him, he galloped towards the Spanish King.

"To the death, then!" Rodrigo shouted back. Almost as soon as the words were out of his mouth, Tarik's sword plunged through his neck.

Rodrigo died at once, and his body tumbled down from his bejewelled saddle. Startled to find Rodrigo's weight suddenly gone from her back, his horse took fright. As she galloped away, the sun gleamed off her snow-white coat and the jewels of her empty saddle glittered in the rays of the sun.

# Roland and Oliver

"I will never forgive Roland for this, never!" Ganelon muttered as he spurred his horse away from the camp of his commander, the Frankish King Charlemagne. Ganelon felt an enormous desire for revenge. He had always hated Roland, his stepson and the nephew of Charlemagne. Now he hated him more than ever. Because of Roland, Ganelon was riding into great danger, perhaps to his death.

After seven years of victorious war against the Muslims in Spain, Charlemagne had grown weary of fighting. He wanted to make peace with Marsilion of Saragossa, the only Muslim king he had not overcome. Charlemagne decided to send an ambassador to Marsilion and Roland had suggested Ganelon. Charlemagne agreed.

Ganelon was furious, but he had to obey Charlemagne. It was a dangerous mission, for the Muslims were very violent and unpredictable people.

The more Ganelon thought about it, the more he realised that perilous or not, this mission could give him the chance to get his revenge. 'If I can persuade King Marsilion to help me,' Ganelon mused, 'I could get rid of Roland for ever.'

Despite his fears about the dangers of his journey, Ganelon reached Saragossa safely. At first, Marsilion and the Muslims were very suspicious of Ganelon, but eventually they agreed to cooperate with him. In any case, the Muslims, too, wanted revenge, for they had suffered many dreadful defeats at the hands of the Franks.

"You must send hostages to Charlemagne, to show that you truly mean to make peace," Ganelon advised Marsilion.

Marsilion agreed to do so, and Ganelon went on: "When Charlemagne has your hostages, he will take his army home. However, he will not leave himself unprotected as he marches through the narrowest passes of the mountains of the Pyrenees. The pass at Roncevaux is particularly dangerous. I am sure that Charlemagne will leave a force of his soldiers there to guard it.''

"How will that help you get rid of your stepson Roland?'' King Marsilion asked curiously.

"You will see,'' Ganelon replied with a wicked smile. "Just make sure your men are well hidden behind the rocks around the pass. I will do the rest.''

When Ganelon returned with the Muslim hostages and the news that Marsilion was willing to make peace, Charlemagne at once made preparations to return home. Charlemagne's great army set off, and moved slowly through the Pyrenees. There were great, soaring peaks on either side and only narrow, winding mountain trails to follow. Their progress was slow, and the rumblings and clatterings of their carts could be heard a long way off. Marsilion's men heard the noise as they raced ahead to Roncevaux. As long as they kept the noise behind them, they knew they would reach Roncevaux before the Franks got there.

So it proved. When the Frankish army reached Roncevaux, Marsilion's force lay concealed from view behind the rocks and in the crevices of the surrounding mountains.

"This is a perilous place,'' Charlemagne announced, just as Ganelon had guessed he would. "I will leave twenty thousand knights to guard the pass as my army moves through.'' Charlemagne looked round. "Who will command this rearguard?'' he asked.

At once, before anyone else could speak, Ganelon came forward and said, "Roland, Sire. Put Roland in command. He well deserves so important a task.''

Out of the corner of his eye, Ganelon saw Roland's face light up with excitement at his stepfather's suggestion. However, Charlemagne did not agree at first.

"Roland is a splendid soldier, but he is too young and rash,'' the King replied. "It needs an older, more experienced man.''

At this, Roland threw himself to his knees in front of Charlemagne.

"I beg you, Sire,'' Roland cried. "Give me this command. I swear I will prove worthy of it. I will defend the pass here at Roncevaux with my very life if I must.''

Ganelon begged Charlemagne, "Heed my stepson's request, gracious sire. After all, Roland honoured me with a great task, as ambassador to King Marsilion. I would return the favour."

Confronted by Ganelon's insistence and Roland's eagerness, Charlemagne at last gave in.

"Very well, then," he said, "but Oliver and the Twelve Peers will remain behind with Roland."

Oliver was Roland's sensible and stout-hearted friend. The Twelve Peers were the bravest and most experienced Frankish knights. Charlemagne hoped that between them they could stop Roland from doing anything foolish. And if they were in danger, Roland could always blow his horn and summon Charlemagne and his army to his aid.

When Charlemagne and his army had moved off, Roland set about disposing his forces. Some he set to guard the pass itself, others he sent to watch on the mountain ridges above.

The Muslims lay low until they were sure Charlemagne was some distance away. Then, all at once, Roland and Oliver were startled to hear the sound of a thousand trumpets echoing through the mountains. The sound echoed back and forth between the peaks, and before the echo had died away, there came the sound of horses galloping and the fearful war cries of the Muslim hordes.

Oliver scrambled up a steep rise by the side of the path, to a point where he could scan the ground on the other side. There, to his horror, he saw the great mass of Marsilion's warriors. Thousands of burnished helmets gleamed in the mountain sunshine. Thousands of spears, shields and swords glinted menacingly in the clear bright light. All of them were moving rapidly towards the pass at Roncevaux. Oliver hurried down to where Roland was standing.

"There are at least one hundred thousand of them," he told Roland fearfully. "We will be overwhelmed. I beg you, Roland, sound your horn now. Summon Charlemagne back!"

Oliver was appalled when Roland refused. "I will summon no aid," Roland maintained stubbornly. "If we cannot throw back the Muslims ourselves, we deserve to die as cowards!"

A terrible despair took hold of Oliver. Charlemagne had been right not to want the incautious Roland to command his rearguard. Twice more, Oliver begged Roland to summon Charlemagne. Twice more, Roland refused. It was too late now, in any case. Marsilion's Muslims were thundering closer and closer. There was nothing to do but confront them and fight to the death.

A few moments later, the Muslims were upon them. Roland and his knights plunged into the battle, slashing about them with their swords and spears.

Roland drove his spear through a Muslim's shield and helmet with one mighty thrust. Then he forced his way into a group of Muslims and brought down fifteen of them before the shaft of his spear broke into pieces. Undaunted, Roland grasped Durendal, his great sword, and flung himself towards a Muslim warrior. He killed the man and his horse with one swift stroke.

Before long, few Muslims remained alive. The rest had fallen before the thrusting spears, slashing swords and hammering blows of the Franks. Although many of his own men had also been killed, Roland was sure that he had won a great victory. He was just about to raise Durendal to proclaim his triumph when, suddenly, the sound of trumpets reached his ears.

Instantly, Roland knew what it was. "A second Muslim army!" he gasped.

Seconds later, the slopes above the pass at Roncevaux seemed to be covered in a fresh crowd of Muslim warriors. Like a great tide, they swamped down on to Roland and the exhausted, battle-stained survivors of his force.

Roland and the Franks hurled themselves against this new, mighty enemy, but they were soon close to being overwhelmed. One Muslim killed five of the Twelve Peers, another two Peers fell and soon only sixty Frankish knights were left alive.

Roland looked round at the bodies of his men littering the ground. At last, he realised he must blow his horn and summon Charlemagne. Roland's horn was covered in gold and precious stones and its high clear note could be heard further away than any other horn in the world.

Roland put the mouthpiece of the horn to his lips, but Oliver rushed up and stopped him.

"It would be to our dishonour if you called for help now!" Oliver shouted angrily. "Better to die here than live in disgrace!"

"No, I MUST summon Charlemagne now," Roland replied. "If I had listened to you and done so before, this disaster would never have happened."

Before Oliver could say any more, Roland put the horn to his lips and blew with all the strength he possessed. Harder and harder he blew until, suddenly, he felt a snap and a dreadful pain in his head. All at once, blood was flowing from his mouth. Roland had blown with such force that a vein in the side of his head had burst.

The sound of the horn soared up into the sky and over the mountains, echoing on and on until it reached the ears of Charlemagne, thirty leagues away. Charlemagne started up in his saddle in great alarm.

"Dear God!" he cried. "Roland has been attacked!" Charlemagne turned

the head of his horse to ride back swiftly to Roland's aid. "Pray God we may reach him in time," he muttered fearfully.

Ganelon, hearing this, gave a derisive laugh. "Do not trouble yourself, Sire!" he scoffed. "It is only one of Roland's tricks. There is no attack. Come, let us get on – we are far from home."

In that moment, Charlemagne realised what Ganelon had done.

"You have betrayed Roland! You have betrayed me!" the King roared. "Seize him!" he ordered.

A group of Frankish knights, as infuriated as Charlemagne at Ganelon's treachery, leapt upon him, bound him and flung him into one of the baggage carts.

"You shall die for this foul betrayal!" Charlemagne promised Ganelon. Charlemagne kept his promise, for Ganelon was afterwards put to death.

Quickly, the whole Frankish army turned and headed back the way it had come. They rode as fast as the rocky terrain and the winding mountain paths would allow them. From time to time, the Franks heard Roland's horn echoing across the mountains. Charlemagne's trumpeters blew in reply.

A night and a day passed before they could be heard at Roncevaux.

The Muslims, seeing Charlemagne was returning, fled in panic. They left Charlemagne to discover a dreadful scene of tragedy and death.

The battlefield at Roncevaux was thickly littered with the corpses of men and horses. Oliver lay dead, his face ghostly white. A Muslim spear had struck him in the back and pierced right through his body to his chest. All twelve Peers had been killed. As he looked slowly round, Charlemagne realised that all the knights he had left with Roland were lying dead before him.

Then the grieving King of the Franks found Roland. He was lying on a grassy bank close to a rock. Upon the rock, Charlemagne saw three deep sword-cuts. Beneath Roland's body lay his beautiful bejewelled horn and his sword Durendal. Knowing that he was dying, for he had lost so much blood from continuously blowing his horn, Roland had tried to destroy Durendal by striking it on the rock. Durendal had remained unbroken, however, and Roland had not had the strength to try a fourth time. Instead, to keep Durendal from falling into Muslim hands, Roland had placed it on the ground. Then he had lain upon it, and there, he had died.

Charlemagne tore his beard with grief. He wept and called out the names of his dead knights. He swore he would have his revenge. As it was nearly dark now, Charlemagne knelt and prayed that the sun would stand still in the sky so that he could pursue the fleeing Muslims. Charlemagne's prayer was granted. Only when he and his army had killed all the Muslims and left their bodies strewn along the road to Saragossa or in the river nearby, did the sun set and the night fall.

# El Cid

In the summer of 1099, a great sadness filled the city of Valencia in Spain. People walked through the streets, heads down, hardly exchanging a word with each other. There was none of the normal, cheerful chatter and noise in the markets. At the inns, men sat drinking their tankards of wine or beer in melancholy silence. The innkeepers, who were usually full of good stories and good cheer, had no tales or jokes to tell; they went about their work with long, morose faces.

If anyone asked a question, it was always the same one: 'Any news yet?' The reply might be 'No' or simply a sad shake of the head. What the people of Valencia feared most was the day when the answer to that question would be 'Yes'. That would mean that El Cid, Roderigo Diaz de Vivar, ruler of Valencia, was dead.

El Cid was an old man, worn out by more than thirty years of fighting battles and hard campaigning. With his armies, El Cid had marched long gruelling distances in the burning heat of the Spanish summer. Many times he had been wounded, only to ignore his injuries and inspire his men by fighting alongside them. Now all those years of hardship had taken their toll. El Cid was dying. Worse still for the people of Valencia, their Muslim enemies were gleefully anticipating his death, for then they could make their final attack on Valencia and capture it.

The Muslims had themselves given Roderigo Diaz his nickname of 'El Cid'. In Arabic, the Muslim language, it meant 'Lord'. Roderigo's own Christian armies had another name for him: 'Campeador', which meant 'winner of battles'. Both Muslims and Christians agreed that El Cid was the greatest soldier in Spain. At a time when the two sides were struggling for control of the country, the armies led by El Cid had prevailed in one battle after another, and helped Christian rule to spread through northern Spain. After 1094, El Cid had conquered and ruled a large area of eastern Spain, in the province of Valencia.

El Cid was so successful that Muslim soldiers used to tremble if they even heard his name. Their leaders came to realise they could never win victories over the Christians while El Cid lived. So the Muslims bided their time and early in 1099 the news they most wanted to hear reached them. El Cid's health was failing. He was too weak to rise from his bed except for short periods of time. His faithful and beautiful wife, Jimena, spent most of her time at his bedside. She was afraid that if she left him, even for a few moments, he might die in her absence and she would be robbed of the chance to say her final farewell.

There was great rejoicing in the Muslims' camp when this became known. At once, the Muslim army began to gather, ready to attack as soon as El Cid breathed his last.

El Cid knew what was happening and he felt great frustration and fury. 'What can I do?' he thought. 'My people depend on me, and I am too sick to help them . . .'

129

El Cid shuddered as he realised what would happen once he was dead. It was easy to picture the scene – the ferocious Muslims sweeping through the streets, killing men, women and children, setting fire to the houses, destroying the churches and seizing all the treasure in the city.

"Somehow, I must save my people, I must!" El Cid murmured.

Day by day, El Cid grew weaker. All the time, he struggled with the problem. At last, when he was almost too ill to think clearly any more, he decided on a plan. He told Jimena to call his captains to his bedside, and when they came, he told them what he wanted them to do.

Then El Cid looked at Jimena. "When I die, do not weep for me," he told her. Jimena, already in tears, nodded her head. "No one must know I am dead," El Cid whispered. "Not for a while, at least. Above all, the Muslims must not know it. Promise me, all of you, that you will do as I have commanded."

"Yes, yes, we will," Jimena replied. "Everything shall be done as you wish, my beloved husband."

El Cid smiled. "Then Valencia will be saved," he said.

A few hours later, El Cid died. Jimena kissed him for the last time, then got to her feet, pale and red-eyed, but calm.

"You know what you must do now," Jimena told the captains. Then she hurried away to order the soldiers in Valencia to arm themselves and prepare for war.

"Beat the drums for battle!" Jimena ordered. "El Cid is coming to lead you to another great victory over the Muslims!"

The soldiers were mystified at first. This was the last thing they had expected. But they decided that El Cid must have recovered from his sickness, and was at this moment putting on his armour and his trusty sword called Tizona. The soldiers became certain that this was so when they saw El Cid's white horse, Bavieca, being led from its stable and saddled.

Outside Valencia, the Muslims heard the drums beating and the clank of arms and armour inside the city. They heard the sudden cheering of crowds of people who surged into the streets to greet the columns of El Cid's soldiers as they moved towards the city gates.

"What's this?" the Muslims cried, alarmed and surprised. "Have the Christians gone mad? El Cid must be dead by now, yet they are cheering and joyful."

At once, the Muslims scrambled to prepare for battle. They had managed to get into their armour, grab their swords and spears and form up their battle lines when the great gates of Valencia swung slowly open. A single horseman galloped out, holding in one hand a large white banner with a brilliant red cross emblazoned on it. In his other hand, he held a mighty sword. Behind him, hundreds of horsemen were followed by a huge crowd of foot soldiers.

The lone horseman galloped closer, until he was near enough for the Muslims to recognise.

"It's El Cid!" they yelled in sudden fear. "El Cid is leading his army against us!"

It was undoubtedly El Cid. Every Muslim in Spain could recognise that stern face, that unwavering soldierly gaze and the tall, upright figure of the general who had conquered them over and over again. And behind him came what seemed like an enormous army. At least 70,000 men, or so the Muslims thought.

As the Christians came thundering towards them, the Muslims heard every man chanting, "Cid! Cid! Cid!" At the sound of this name, the Muslim soldiers panicked. They began to run, and their horsemen, likewise, turned and started to gallop away. Before long, the entire Muslim army was in flight, running away as fast as they could with the Christians in pursuit.

At last, when El Cid's captains were certain that the Muslims would not come back, they ordered their men to return to Valencia. They marched back, singing and yelling, to be greeted by wildly cheering crowds as they entered the city.

No one noticed that one of the captains had remained behind holding on to the bridle of El Cid's horse Bavieca.

"This last victory is your greatest victory, my Lord Cid," the captain murmured, gazing at the stiff, unmoving figure sitting upright in Bavieca's saddle.

In all the excitement, no one, either Christian or Muslim, had seen that El Cid was firmly lashed into the saddle so that he could not fall off. The arms holding the banner and the sword were propped up by shafts of wood concealed beneath the sleeves of his chain-mail tunic. These had been El Cid's orders – that his captains dress him in his armour and place him on Bavieca's back so that he could lead his army into battle even after he was dead. By this means, El Cid put heart into his own men and fear into the Muslims. He succeeded brilliantly.

The captain pulled Bavieca's bridle and made the horse turn round. Then he led Bavieca, with the dead Cid sitting on its back, away from Valencia. He was heading inland, into the Kingdom of Castile and the city of Burgos. There, El Cid had been born and there, according to his own orders, he wanted to be buried.

# William Tell

"Hey, you! Come back at once, unless you want to be killed on the spot!"

William Tell knew that voice. It was harsh and loud. It sounded as if it belonged to a cruel man. Gritting his teeth with anger, William Tell went on striding across the square.

"Stop, I said!" roared the voice. "Or I swear I'll . . . "

William halted and turned on his heel. He glared across the square at Vogt Gessler, the fat, evil-looking man to whom the voice belonged. William's fingers tightened around the shaft of the crossbow he carried in his hand. How he longed to shoot one good bolt straight into Gessler's black heart!

Vogt Gessler, the Austrian governor of the Swiss canton of Uri, was a tyrant. Seven hundred years ago, the freedom-loving Swiss were over-ruled by Austrians. As a result, they hated all Austrians, but Gessler most of all. Gessler delighted in making the people of Uri suffer as much as possible. He sent his men to steal their food and turn them out of their homes. He took their money, or he imprisoned them and beat them for no reason at all. The man was a fiend, with a soul as black as hell.

Now the latest humiliation Gessler imposed upon the people was a hat set upon a pole in the centre of the town square at Altdorf. Gessler had proclaimed that this was the symbol of the mighty power of the Austrians, and everyone had to kneel before it.

The pole, with the ridiculous hat perched on top of it, stood only a short way from where William Tell stood now. He had walked right past it, for he absolutely refused to kneel before that or any other symbol of Austrian power.

Gessler was swaggering across the square towards him. "You swear to do what, Gessler?" William snarled as the Austrian approached. "Kill me? Put me in prison? You would have a riot on your hands within the hour! Remember who I am, Gessler – and take care!"

Gessler knew who William Tell was all right! He was the greatest hero and the finest bowman in all Switzerland. Everyone, not just the people in the canton of Uri, looked up to him. Gessler knew that if he laid a finger on William Tell, there were scores of Swiss who would be glad to kill him in order to avenge their hero.

Gessler decided to ignore William's words. Instead, he pointed to the pole in the square.

"You have been ordered to kneel before that hat!" the Austrian growled. "You walked past it. This is an insult to the Emperor!"

William laughed. "The Emperor? That miserable creature! I would not let a hair of my head bend in honour to him."

Gessler began to get angry. "Kneel before that hat!" he shouted. "I command you!"

"Never!" William replied stubbornly.

Before the infuriated Gessler could reply, William turned and stalked off – his head held high. Gessler watched the proud, straight-backed figure of the Swiss bowman and cursed and swore under his breath.

The impudence of the man, the sheer impudence! This was not the first time William Tell had openly defied Gessler and the Austrians.

"It must stop!" Gessler raged. "I must find some way to get the better of him."

For days afterwards, Gessler brooded over one plan after another. At last, the very idea he wanted came into his head. "What a splendid revenge I shall have!" Gessler chortled.

Gessler grabbed a quill pen and two pieces of parchment. On one parchment, he wrote a short, urgent message to his friend, the Governor of Zurich. On the second parchment, Gessler wrote out a proclamation.

That same afternoon, Gessler's proclamation, signed and sealed with a splendid red wax seal, appeared on the door of the church in Altdorf. At once, people began crowding round, wondering what the black-hearted Gessler wanted to inflict upon them now.

However, the proclamation contained no orders. Instead, it contained a challenge.

'Walther of Zurich, the greatest crossbowman in the world, arrives in Altdorf in three days' time,' Gessler had written. 'It is well known that no Swiss bowman can match Walther for skill and accuracy with the crossbow, but any Swiss foolish enough to challenge him may do so. The people of Altdorf and all Switzerland will then see how puny their men are compared to a mighty Austrian warrior like Walther! So that all in Altdorf may witness Walther's triumph, men, women and children are commanded to attend the contest in the square under pain of death!'

The people of Uri were infuriated by the insult in the proclamation. They rushed to William Tell to inform him of the contest. It was quite unnecessary, Gessler realised, to threaten everyone in Altdorf with death unless they attended, for everyone would want to come. Gessler just wanted to make sure, though, that William Tell brought his small son with him. That was a very important part of the plan.

Three days later, the entire population of Altdorf gathered in the town square. Gessler arrived with Walther, who had come speedily from Zurich. The Austrian was a large man, with great muscle-bound arms. Hc was an extremely good shot and the best crossbowman in the Austrian army. The people of Altdorf, naturally, believed that William Tell was much better and they looked forward to seeing Walther well and truly beaten.

Walther positioned himself in the centre of the square, and when a fanfare of trumpets blew, the crowd fell silent. Gessler stepped forward.

"Who comes to challenge the best crossbowman in the world?" he cried. "Does anyone dare?"

At once, William Tell came out into the square, crossbow in hand. "I dare!" he cried in ringing tones. "Show me the target, and I will show you how a crossbow should be used. Come, what is the target?"

This was the moment Gessler had been waiting for. He nodded to three soldiers whom he had stationed close by. Before anyone could stop them they pushed into the crowd, grabbed William Tell's young son and pulled him out into the square.

"What is this, Gessler?" cried William. "What evil trick are you playing?"

Gessler smiled grimly. "You asked what the target was!" he said, pointing to William's son. "The target is your own child!"

At this, screams and wails of shock and amazement sounded in the crowd. William Tell turned very pale. He knew he could not back down from the challenge now. That would bring him great dishonour. But to shoot at his own son! It was Gessler's most fiendish plot yet.

"You devil, Gessler! You shall roast in Hell for this!" William cried. He was trembling violently – half with fear, half with rage.

"I think not," Gessler said. "I am not asking you to shoot towards him. See!" Gessler pulled a large red apple out of his pocket. "This is what you shall aim for. This apple will be placed on your son's head. If you are as good a crossbowman as people say, you and your son should have nothing to fear. But if not . . . " Gessler chuckled wickedly. He had no need to say any more. wickedly. He had no need to say any more.

Still trembling, William Tell took the apple and placed it carefully on top of the boy's fair hair.

"Keep very still, my dearest boy," he whispered to him. "Do not flinch. Do not move, for if you do, my aim cannot be true!"

The boy attempted to smile.

"I will try, Father," he said in a small, frightened voice.

William kissed the boy farewell. Praying hard that fear of killing him would not spoil his aim, he walked slowly back across the square. A line had been marked for the crossbowmen, and William put his foot on it. He raised his crossbow, and with tremendous effort managed to hold it steady. He took aim.

Everyone in the square had their eyes glued on William Tell – including Gessler.

'He will be too afraid to shoot straight,' Gessler thought gleefully. 'His son is sure to die!'

William looked along the shaft of his crossbow. he saw his son's small, frightened face staring at him and started to tremble. He struggled to control himself. Slowly, William raised the crossbow until the shaft and the bolt inside it were in line with the apple on top of his son's head. A second later, William pulled the bowstring and then swiftly closed his eyes. He could not bear to watch.

William Tell need not have worried. His aim was as perfect as always. The bolt sped through the air and plunged straight into the apple. It fell apart, in two neat, clean halves.

A tremendous cheer went up from the crowd and people began running across the square to congratulate William on his amazing marksmanship. They reached him to find him sobbing with relief.

Gessler was furious. His plan had failed completely. He turned and began to stalk angrily away from the square, taking Walther with him. Before he had gone far, William Tell called to him.

"Gessler! See this!" he cried. Gessler looked, to see William holding a second crossbow bolt in his hand. "If I had killed my son, Vogt Gessler," he growled at the Austrian, "this bolt would have entered your wicked heart! Here – take it." William tossed the bolt towards Gessler, who jumped back quickly in case it hit him. The crowd laughed. "Keep it as a souvenir of this contest," William shouted as Gessler stalked away. "I have plenty more, and I swear that on the day we Swiss drive the Austrians out of Switzerland, one of them will be specially reserved for you!"